Nightcry

by

Gregory M. Thompson

This is a work of fiction. All characters, organizations and events portrayed in this book are the products of the author's imagination.

NIGHTCRY

A Trembles Press Book

www.nightcrynovel.com

ISBN: 978-1-4609-3670-2

Cover Art by Luke Imbery
©2011

For Nancy –

you know all the reasons

CHAPTER ONE

1

It was near Horse Creek I found the woman's body, embedded in the bank. She lied there arms out and legs open, as if interrupted while in the process of making dirt angels. The woman wore no clothes and I glanced about to see if they had fallen off or had been ripped off and thrown aside. She rested face up and from what I could tell she was maybe fifty or sixty—possibly older from the sag of her breasts.

Caked blood hung around her ears like morbid earrings. Most of the skin had decayed, wrinkled like the face of a Pug. The pallid skin appeared very loose, ready to fall from the body at a slight touch or a small vibration on the ground underneath. I would not be the one testing *that* theory—I had no desire to watch skin slide like epidermis syrup. It was bad enough I stood this close to the body without puking or—at the very least—getting an upset stomach. But I hadn't had that much to eat the night before, so I remained confident I'd be okay.

I quickly wondered how long this body had been here. Days? Weeks? Months? I realized this spot was not well-traveled, but shouldn't someone have reported her missing?

2

Police Chief Hardass (or Bobby Hamilton, if you prefer proper names) withdrew from his car as he always did: spouting arrogance. The cockiness was unwarranted. So what if he was six and a half feet and 220 pounds of muscle? The Police Chief title gave him the right of absolute domain over assholedom in these parts, but what was there to be proud of, watching over a community of six hundred law-abiding citizens?

He made his last arrest two months ago on Old Man Noogan who drank a bit too much that day and ran over Miss Molly's cat. Hamilton only charged Noogan with animal cruelty despite the entire incident being a clear accident. How's that for showcasing your power? Now all he does was patrol the streets of Ilton and speak on the hazards of drugs at the local high school.

Besides me, Hamilton was the only one of my class that stayed. Everyone else got real jobs and made something of themselves in Chicago or New York or San Francisco or where ever people made something of themselves. Little old me was in charge of the Ilton Gazette and Bobby Hamilton was in charge of being an asshole. Technically, I attempted to make something of myself but I eventually returned to my hometown to run a twelve-page paper and endure the boundless ineptitude of the Police Chief.

Bobby nodded to me as he approached. "Grant."

"Chief." It's hard calling a classmate, who is the same twenty-eight years as you, 'Chief'.

"What have we got here?"

I pointed to the body. "I found that body there about 20 minutes ago."

"Mmm-hmm." Bobby walked over to the body and knelt down. He took a pencil from his breast pocket and poked around the woman, focused on a few of the cuts and gashes. I watched him carefully lift leaves and push tufts of grass around, searching for evidence, but after a few minutes of that, he gave up. He rose and very rudely stepped over the midsection of the body and stared straight ahead.

"You found her like this? You didn't touch anything?" He finally asked.

"That's gross, man."

"So you found her like this?" he asked, forceful.

"Yes."

"Mmm-hmm."

I felt my cheeks burning when he said 'Mmm-hmm'. Condescending, really. He stood back up and glanced around the scene.

"County coroner's coming," he said. "'Bout 30 minutes." That's about how long anybody took to get out here. Kankakee wasn't just a hop, skip and a jump. No one visited here willingly. You have to *plan* to come to Ilton.

Grant picked up the woman's wrist and checked the pulse.

"Dead," he said.

"Obviously."

"She look familiar?"

I hadn't recognized her the first time I saw her, but I hadn't really *looked*. I would have to force myself again, but I wanted out of here, so I looked at her face.

The eye cavities sunk back into the skull, leaving the eyes to protrude outward, like a surprised skeleton. Old, matted hair dipped across the forehead, almost thinning to the point of non-existence. Another few days or so and the facial bones would push through, saying a little hello to anyone else who looked on her.

"Well?" Bobby pressed. With a latex-gloved hand, Bobby put his index finger on the woman's chin and opened the lower jaw. Immediately, maggots and a couple of spiders and other multi-footed animals shot out, escaping from the toothy prison for a brighter day.

I looked away, a queasy rumble emanating from my stomach. A short second later, my abdomen lurched upward, pushing a dry heave through my mouth.

Bobby released a short burst of chuckles. "Everything okay?"

"I'm fine," I responded. I managed a swallow.

"I'm guessing she doesn't look familiar to you."

"No," I said. "But that doesn't mean she couldn't be from one of these farmhouses. I don't know too many of those folks."

"Not familiar to me either."

"Listen, mind if I get going—"

"What were you doing out here?"

"Camping."

Bobby snickered. "Camping? I didn't know anybody camped out here."

"Been doing it since I was seven."

"How far away?"

I looked past a clump of trees. "I don't know. About 500 feet or so."

"Hear anything last night?"

"No." And come to think of it, I really hadn't.

"Only reason I ask is that this probably happened sometime in the night. You out here all night?"

I nodded. "Since around 10 p.m. or so."

"Mmm-hmm."

There it was again. His asshole 'Mmm-hmm'.

"Show me," he said.

"Show you what?"

"Show me your campsite."

"Fine."

We followed the creek until the treeline began. Rain blanketed the area with a light drizzle early this morning and the banks became mushy as a result. Hamilton's shiny police boots collected mud and I loved it.

The forest enclosed us within a few steps of entering the forest floor. An abrupt temperature drop shook my bones and with each step, I hoped the moisture wouldn't seep into my shoes. Inside the trees, it was hard to ascertain whether this was the early spring season— where the melting show or early March/April rains soaked everything—or the middle of the Fall season—where the forty or fifty degree days just made things blustery.

The trip was not a direct shot to my campsite. Bobby and I zigzagged through the evergreens and an occasional thorn bush grabbed at us while trying to avoid overly-damp areas.

When we reached a drier area, Bobby stopped me. "Hold on."

"See something?" I asked.

Instead of answering, he bent down and grabbed a handful of leaves and grass. He used that to wipe the clumpy mud from his boots. I shook my head and continued on.

I saw my grey, two-man tent a few moments later. I left the flap open and hoped there weren't any animals milling around in there—like a raccoon or a field mouse. Or worse, a coyote. The past few weeks, farmers have reported more coyotes than in the past five years. I witnessed one personally last year. It was skinny, bones pushing through the fur and it's eyes and stomach hungry for a kill.

"That it?" Bobby asked.

"Who else's would it be?"

He cautiously approached it first. He popped his head inside the tent and—seeing everything was okay—relaxed. He waved his hand at the defunct fire. "You know a fire's illegal on private property," he said.

"Is that all you're concerned about? You got a dead lady back there, you know."

Maybe I made a mistake saying that last thing. Bobby stomped over to me and tapped my shoulder with his finger.

"Listen here, Grant. I know we went to school together and we graduated together and that we've been stuck in this God-awful town since and we'll probably be stuck here for many years yet, but don't you think for one fucking second that you can treat me like an idiot." His voice quivered at the end, but he regained his thoughts and continued. "I know I wasn't the smartest guy in school, but I kinda made something here as Police Chief. I'm *proud* of this town. I'm horribly sick to my stomach about having a dead body on my watch."

I took a step back. "Okay, okay. Just didn't know why you're worried about a stupid fire, anyway."

"Did you leave the campsite at any time last night?" Back to the questioning.

"No."

"What did you do?"

"I made a fire. I made dinner. Then I read a book until I went to sleep."

"What did you have for dinner?" he asked.

"Some sandwiches. Bologna and Cheese."

Bobby looked around the campsite. "You didn't litter out here, did you? I mean, what did you do with the little plastic baggies you put your sandwiches in?"

"Fuck you, Hamilton. I used Tupperware." If he looked inside, I'm sure he'd see them.

"Were you camping by yourself?"

"Yup. Felt like I needed to get away for the weekend."

Hamilton laughed. "The big city, right? Ilton getting you down?"

"No, but you are. What's your problem?"

"We got plenty of time before the coroner gets here. Besides, you do realize you were only 500 feet or so away from the scene of the crime, right? Don't tell me being editor has warped your brain."

"I didn't do anything." I tried not to sound defensive with the heat of anger ready to control my mouth.

"Mmm-hmm." Dammit! I wanted to take that 'Mmm-hmm' and shove it up his ass!

Bobby started walking back the way we came. "I suppose I need to check the scene out."

"Yeah, I suppose."

He jerked his head back to me, but didn't say anything. He wanted to, I saw his eyes flare.

4

Of course, he didn't.

Instead, he walked up to the bridge and looked both ways. Probably be another 10 minutes or so before the Coroner came.

"Need a ride, Grant?"

"No. I'll walk back."

"Will you be at the office all day?"

"It's Monday."

"Is that a yes or no? I don't know your schedule."

"Yes."

"Talk to you later, then."

That sounded like we were good old friends. No, not good old friends: the *bestest* friends in the whole wide world. *Talk to you later, then.* Fucking Hamilton.

The walk took me fifteen minutes, which calmed me. Police Chief Bobby Hamilton had pissed me off and I needed to clear my head before the day's editing took place. The *Ilton Gazette* was published every Tuesday and each Monday I had to look over the proofs, write my editorial and do any last minute print settings. I know: sounds pretty damn boring and it was. But I got it down to a science where I can be done by one p.m., two at the latest.

The rest of the week was reserved for the fun stuff, like writing about my find along the creek this morning.

I reached Main Street and wondered if the Coroner was there, checking things out, making shit official. Probably. Unless he stopped off for a quickie with Harriet Miller, the Mayor's daughter. Mayor Miller. Now doesn't that have a nice ring to it? Mayor Miller. He's been Mayor for over ten years and was the only person who didn't know Coroner Fergins was banging his daughter. Oh, and maybe Bobby. If Fergins stopped off for that quickie, then he might not be there yet. Or, maybe Fergins followed that nickname for sex and really was quick. I don't know the man, but he was pushing fifty.

9:15. Shit. The peons were wondering about me.

I quickened my pace and walked by *Betty's Grubs*, the local greasy spoon. The scent of scrambled eggs and waffles drifted out and slammed my nose. Maybe a fast detour and I could grab myself a quickie of breakfast—

"Grant! Grant!"

I didn't have to look. It was my Ad-man, Joe Griffin. He trotted in my direction. Joe was the stereotypical short, stocky, bald man. I could see the rolls of fat jiggling under his dress shirt and wished for a different image.

—I thought of Harriet's boobs—

Better. Just a few years older than me, she still had some great tits.

"Grant, where've you been?"

His fat pushed Harriet's boobs from my mind.

Finally, Joe reached me. I waited for him to catch his breath before speaking again.

"Worried about…you…"

"Want some breakfast?" I knew he wouldn't turn down food.

"Not really." Was this a short, stocky, bald man who didn't want food? That surprised me. "We've got a problem with an advertiser."

"Do I have time for breakfast?"

"Not if you want to get the paper out on time."

And if there's one thing I wanted to do, it's just that.

6

"So what's the problem?" I asked my staff of four.

Maggie Johnson sat closest to me and chewed on a pen. Who chewed on a pen? Pencils were the thing; the little wood divots made the habit satisfying. I guess Maggie enjoyed the threat of spewing ink. Her long, red hair streaked back into a pony tail, opening the view to her smooth, tanned face. My eyes were too wanton at the moment; a small stirring shifted in my pants. My eyes wandered to her skirt and to her perfect legs; then out of courtesy, I lifted my eyes back up to her face. She smiled at me. She knew, but she smiled anyway.

"…And that's why he won't purchase the rest of the ad space."

How rude of me. "Who won't? I'm sorry, I only half heard."

"Alan's Auto," Daryl Benton said. He was my community guy. Usually drunk at night, but he's able to sniff out the tiniest bit of story in this area during the day. If a tractor had a flat tire because of a nail that a neighbor had deliberately set in the road, then Daryl was *the* guy to get to the bottom of it. And sometimes that's the biggest story we had for the week. He took off his glasses and set them down on his notebook. "Alan's Automotive doesn't think he's getting the response he should from his ad. He feels another four inches of space won't help."

The sports man, Pete Folly, finished typing something and spun it out of the typewriter. That's right, *typewriter*. Damn guy refuses to submit to the wonders of computer word processing. He's forty and it's slightly strange he hasn't embraced the awe that is Microsoft. He set the paper on my desk. The title: **ILTON HIGH DEFEATED FOR 4TH STRAIGHT**. Another loss for our hometown basketball team.

"Looks like no State for our boys, eh Pete?" I wondered if my comment would rile him. Some days it was hard to read Pete's mood.

He shrugged.

"What do you think?" I asked Pete when he turned away. "Is Alan getting his worth?"

Pete shrugged again. "Couldn't tell you. I take my car to town when it needs repairing." By town, he meant Kankakee.

I thought for a moment as the penetrating eyes of my employees sought the salvation of an answer. "Joe, offer Alan that extra space free for two weeks. Tell him if his business doesn't improve by 25%, then nothing lost. If it *does* improve, then he must buy two months worth of ads."

Joe smiled. "Like a bet, eh?"

"A friendly business wager."

I caught Pete shaking his head. "Crafty, boss." He plopped back at his desk and started typing again. *Clickety-click-click-click.*

Pete never liked that I took over the paper after the previous editor passed away. Heart attack, or something with his heart. Most days, Pete was pleasant enough, but sometimes— in the things he says—I usually sensed bitterness. I suppose I understood. With Pete, though, he had a shot. First, he was writing obituaries and trying to put himself through school, and then he's working more and more just to stay afloat and soon, the scholastic opportunity passed him by and now he was resigned to move back to his hometown and cover pissy little high school games because without an actual degree, he wasn't just not good enough for Head Honcho. That could have been me three years ago.

The door creaked open and Bobby strolled in. He took off his hat. "How ya doin' Maggie?"

She smiled. "Fine, Bobby. Just fine."

I sensed a little more there, but it wasn't my place. Maybe I'll ask her later.

"What brings you by?" I asked.

"Can I talk to you in your office?" he asked.

This got a few strange looks from Joe and Pete, but Maggie kept right on smiling. Definitely something there. Whether it had been acted on or not was hard to tell.

"Sure, sure." I lead Bobby to my office.

7

Bobby shut the door and laid his hat on my desk.

"I thought you said you didn't leave the campsite," he said.

"I didn't leave. Dinner, read, sleep."

"I got a problem with that."

"With my dinner, my reading or my sleeping?"

"Well," he sighed and sat down. "I found a half-eaten bologna and cheese sandwich next to the victim."

"So."

"Isn't that what you had?"

"Yeah."

"But you didn't leave the campsite."

"I didn't. Do you want to go again? My answer will always be I didn't leave the campsite."

Hamilton waited. I knew he wanted me to say more, but there was nothing more to say.

"Then how do you explain it?" he asked.

I shrugged.

"Did you finish your sandwiches in their entirety?"

"I don't remember." Who remembers that shit anyway?

"Well, try. This is part of a murder."

"Am I part of the murder?"

He paused. "For now."

I gave it to good old Bobby Hamilton. He was handling himself like a pro—like he's investigated hundreds of murders and knew exactly what to ask. Perfect questioning. He must have an *Investigating Murders for Dummies* book sitting on his shelves at home.

"Do I need a lawyer?" I asked him.

"Do you?"

I peeked at his eyes and I knew he wasn't going away until he was satisfied. "Look, I don't know if I ate the whole thing. Maybe I threw it on the ground and some animal carried it off and decided the body might taste better."

He nodded. "Maybe." He stood up. "Thanks for your time."

"Did you get an I.D. on the woman yet?"

"Not yet," he said. "Probably within the hour."

"Can you keep me posted? For the paper?"

Bobby sized me up, trying to affirm some suspicion. "Sure, Grant. But don't get anything out yet. I want this whole thing to go smoothly."

"Anything for you, buddy."

Bobby left amid curious gazes.

Joe was the first one in. "What was that all about?"

"He asked me for advice on the ladies. He's a little shy and small-brained—" I indicated an inch with my thumb and forefinger. "—and asked if it really is the motion of the ocean."

"Right, Right. He looked serious."

"He was. But I can't discuss it yet." I pulled a manila folder from my desk, hoping Joe would take the hint this conversation was done.

"Okay, but is it good?"

"It will increase circulation for the next few weeks."

"Might sell some more ads, huh?" Joe offered.

"Always thinking money. That's what I like."

When Joe left, I flipped open the folder. I needed to proof my editorial. The day was running on and if Bobby kept holding me up, then I may as well publish *next* Tuesday's paper.

I flipped through the folder and couldn't find my editorial. I had the feature, a couple ads to go over, Pete's story and some tidbit pieces, but no editorial.

I checked under the folder, on the floor—

Fuck! I left it in my tent. I worked on it last night.

The clock read 10:30. Half the morning gone and I'd spend the other half getting my article.

"Where you going?" Maggie asked. "Don't we have a paper to put out?"

"I left my editorial at home. Be right back."

I pushed through the door.

8

The body had since been removed and a couple of yellow flags protruded from the ground. *Something important here*, they seemed to say.

I ambled down the side of the bridge and stood by the first flag. Some crumbs were scattered. My damn bologna and cheese sandwich. How the hell did it get here anyway?

I stepped over a string outline of the body and peered down at the second flag. Nothing around it or even near it; just dirt, pebbles, and dying grass. Had I missed something earlier? Or did I even pay attention? Doesn't matter. When it was time to write the story, I'd have to ask Bobby what was at Flag #2.

I made my way through the small forest again. The wind blew through the trees, whooshing through at a snail's pace and whisking ground leaves around and displacing them from any one spot. I heard one bird call out into the air. I paused, hoping the bird received a response. He didn't.

The tent was still erected and the flap remained open. Most of the remnants of the campfire had been blown around. Charred bits of wood littered the area straight west.

Inside the tent, I rummaged around until I found my editorial. Luckily, the pages were intact. Now, back to the office to get this shit done.

As soon as I took one step outside my tent, the wind died down. The bird stopped yakking. Leaves came to a rest. I took another step and didn't hear my feet crunching the ground. Weird.

And through the trees, something blurry rushed by.

CHAPTER TWO

1

More wind, I told myself. The wind got hold of something and blew it right on by.

But the wind wasn't there. It had quit *before* I saw it.

You know you saw it. You're not blind, Grant. You're sharp as a point, mister. How do you think you got to be Editor? What do they say? Eyes like a fucking hawk?

I crept through the trees, keeping my hawk-eyes on the location of the blur. As I reached the creek, I felt some kind of breeze brush my back, caressing my neck hairs in a dreadful way. My body shook in a split-second spasm.

I whirled around and saw nothing.

"Anybody there!?"

Backing up, I tripped over a large rock and landed on my ass. Right in the mud. I stood up and tried to get the mud off, but the stain would be there all day.

Then I looked up.

Floating before me, about 10 feet off the ground was a figure. A woman as far as I could tell. She wore a lace white gown that trailed a few feet behind her. The dress jerked and rippled on her body, if she had one at all. Her deep red hair went down to her butt and flowed outward. Straight and parted in a perfect line in the middle of her head. And since her hair was pulled back, her face was totally revealed.

Her skin was pale and extremely smooth. I don't think I saw a blemish or scar or pock mark at all. Not that I looked for one. She looked Irish, possibly Scottish. Welsh, perhaps, but I wasn't an expert. Oddly pretty, though.

I saw no feet. She bobbed up and down only a few feet away, but always higher up than me.

And she *stared* at me. Right into me. Right through me. My eyes burned, but I couldn't turn my head. I *wanted* to look. Sure I was scared out of my skull, but I couldn't move.

"Hello…" What do you say to a floating woman?

Her only response was a smile. It wasn't a smile of a happy response or a *Hey great to see you* kind of thing. More of a, *I'm a psychopath ready to carve your insides out like a pumpkin and bake them at 350 degrees and gobble them down like I haven't had nothing to eat for a week kind of smile.*

Hers was a wide and gaping smile. Her teeth were like bars, interconnected from top gum to bottom gum with no spaces in between. Each tooth came to a point, which probably were used for easy carving in case she figured me a pumpkin.

Great.

She closed her mouth again, then stopped bobbing and I thought this was it. This was my time and there was nothing I could do about it.

Instead, she floated backwards—and a few feet later—dissipated.

I delayed, but finally got my bearings and sprinted away, still clutching my editorial.

Why hadn't I driven my car? Why the hell had I walked out here?

2

I ran hard back to Ilton and I didn't look back at all.

Running the scenario in my mind took the entire twenty minute trek. What did I see back there? A ghost? I didn't really believe in ghosts, but never counted them out. And if it was a ghost, whose? That woman's?

My stomach flipped like a gymnast thinking about what just happened. I couldn't remember a time I was more scared. The silence, the face, the floating. I could remember sitting in front of the TV watching *Dracula* or *It*

—chewing nails fearful of the clown the vampire squeezing the blanket hoping neither one hid behind me ready to pop up and rip my skin off and scrape out my insides—

but I knew they were movies. I would be frightened for those few hours. Sure, I might have had a nightmare but in a day or two I'd forget about the movie and be on with my days.

But this *really* happened.

No one in town would believe me. I'd be that guy the kids called Crazy. *Hey, Old Crazy Sykes went down by the river, saw a ghost that made him shiver.*

I burst through the doors of the *Ilton Gazette* and tried not to make eye contact as I rushed to the bathroom.

"You okay?" I heard Maggie ask.

I turned both faucets on and looked in the mirror.

Drops of sweat hung like little parachuting men on my face. They dripped on my lips and I tasted the salt as I sucked the little spheres of my excretion into my mouth. They weren't from the walk, I bet. Probably from thinking about that *thing.*

"You're fine, Grant," I said to the mirror. "Just fine."

I splashed some water on my face. That helped. Then I cupped some water in my hand and slurped it. The cool water felt fantastic as it went down my dry throat.

Tell no one. Maybe tomorrow you won't even remember anything. A dream, that's all this was.

I could hope that's what would happen, but a dream it wasn't.

3

Back at my desk, I tried to call Hamilton, but he wasn't in. He's assisting with an autopsy, his secretary said. Do you know when he'll be back? I asked. No, he'll probably grab lunch. Maybe this afternoon.

"I'll call back later," I said and hung up.

Maggie stood in the doorway, quiet

—and floating just like *her*—

with a worried look on her face.

"You okay, Grant?" Concern in her voice.

"Yeah. Rough morning."

"Need to talk about it?"

What? Talk about the ghost that appeared magically in front of me? Tell her it hovered and she had her own wind? Or tell her about the dead body I found and how Hamilton suspects me? So many options. Which one would force her to commit me to the second floor psychiatric ward at the Kankakee Hospital? *Correct*, my mind answered, *all of them*.

"No," I said. "Just want to get the paper out."

"Paper's not as important as you think. If you need to talk, then you should do it. Don't bottle it up and all that shit."

I chuckled. "Do I have to pay you by the hour?"

"Funny. I'm just saying you look flushed. Rattled."

Now was the perfect opportunity to admit the morning's events, but I just couldn't bring myself to tell her. And trust her. Maggie and I were close once—but that was once.

"I'll be fine," I finally said.

"After you finish your stuff, you should go home."

"I'll think about it."

"Is that the best I'm going to get?"

I nodded.

"Okay," she said. "I'll take it."

She spun around and went back to her desk. I checked her ass out the entire way. I feel a little less rattled.

4

My phone rang as I finished my editorial.

"Hello?" I marked the last sentence with my red pen while I held the phone to my ear with my shoulder.

"Grant. It's Bobby."

"Hey. I was trying to get a hold of you earlier."

"I know. Gina told me. I need you to come down to the station."

Station. Isn't that precious. Bobby thought the basement of the community center was a 'station'. "What for? I'm kind of busy right now," I said.

"I want you to identify a couple things and look at the crime scene."

Strange, I thought. Why would the Police Chief need a lowly old editor to look at a crime scene? "Okay," I said, skeptical, but curious. "I'll be there in ten."

He hung up without another word.

On the way out, I told Maggie I'd be at the station for a bit. Joe peered over and said, "Does this have to do with that thing what will sell more ads?"

"That's the only reason I'm going."

Maggie knew something else was up. I'd have to tell her eventually. Maybe tonight. Dinner at my place. Candles. Silk bedsheets for later. Then after the food and passionate sex, I would spill the beans about everything this morning.

—after the passionate sex—

Maybe. After two bouts of sex. I promise.

—two bouts of sex—

I promise.

5

Gina ushered me into the second room of the 'station'. Really, the two rooms were only separated by a corrugated partition that, when opened, combined both of the rooms into one.

Gina's side just had her desk and a few waiting chairs that probably never got their full use. The spotless room smelled like a pumpkin scented candle. A filing cabinet sat in the corner. Bare and boring. I knew they pushed some of the furniture to the side when they needed the basement— like for Community dances, or board meetings, or presentations—but the place could be more lively. Gina could add some flowers or potted trees. Lining the walls with old photographs of the town and people would be cool—anything to make this place lively. I'm sure I could probably locate some black and white pictures in the *Gazette's* archive.

She opened a door section of the partition and pushed me through.

Bobby looked up from a stack of papers. "Grant, thanks for coming." Nice and cordial.

"I'm a little curious, that's all."

Bobby's section of the room rivaled the blandness of the other side. A desk, another filing cabinet that sat behind him and a wastebasket next to his desk half-full of wadded up papers. Behind him on the wall was a single relic of his proudest moment. A 12-foot long black Diamondback rattlesnake had been loose in Ilton about 4 years ago and he had spent the better part of an afternoon corralling the sucker and another two days mounting it. I sometimes think that he enjoyed looking at it and reflecting on that day as his glory. His shining time. The day everyone looked up to him and realized that this guy is our Police Chief and he's the best one in the whole state. I loved small town loyalties and attitudes.

That respect disappeared when a couple of teenagers stole the snake a year ago. They took pictures and held it for ransom. The kids didn't want money for it, they just wanted to give ole Police Chief Bobby Hamilton a hard time. It was hilarious. Did Bobby like the joke? Of course not. Somehow, he got those kids community service for a year.

Bobby stood and took something out of the top drawer of his file cabinet. "Take a look at this," he said.

He set the plastic bag down.

Inside the bag was a brush. It was about nine inches long, and had a four inch or so long handle. The brush was made from silver. I picked the bag up. On the back of the brush were ivy designs that curled around various types of fruit: grapes, apples, peaches, pears. Each piece of fruit had a small clear gem in the center of it.

"Are those diamonds?" I asked.

"Yeah, half carat each."

"And real silver?"

"Yup."

"Was this found at your number 2 flag?"

Bobby looked surprised. "Yes, but how did you know?"

I guessed I should admit what I did. "I went back to the campsite for some newspaper stuff. I walked by the scene."

"You sure you didn't make it a point to go there?"

"I'm sure."

I turned the brush back over. The silver was in good shape—exquisitely polished— though some of the black bristles were broken and bent. Plus, some red hair remained behind.

"Nasty." I commented. Then, something clicked. "Did you have the hairs analyzed?"

"Of course," he said. "It'll be a few days before I get concrete results, but preliminary findings indicate the hair is from someone who passed away years ago."

"Is that possible?"

"The hair is still alive, but some of the cells the guy in Chicago analyzed were from somebody dead."

"Can't be possible."

"Like I said, it's not concrete."

"Think about it, Bobby—"

He shrugged. "That science stuff is not my forte."

"Is that all you brought me down here for? To look at somebody's used comb?"

"Used is an understatement. It's over one hundred years old."

I couldn't tell for sure, but it appeared old. I swear I smelled a musty, stale water odor emanating from the bag.

"Well, lots of people collect antiques," I said.

"But do they let a $500 piece of history lie in the mud?" He snatched back the bag and replaced it in the cabinet.

He had a point to the comb, but I grew tired of sitting here. Was there a point to the visit? I guess I'll try again. "So is that it?"

"No. There's something else." He sat in his chair and sighed. "This is hard for me to say, but I need your help."

"Do you now. And what would the Chief of Police have me do?"

"I knew I shouldn't have brought you down here, but Gina insisted you were the best one to help."

"What do you need?" I asked, resigned to the fact Bobby used a lot of effort calling me down here to ask for my help.

"I want you to keep your eyes and ears open. You're loved in this town. You're a hometown boy. I can admit that the people don't like me as much and that's fine. I'm not doing this job to make friends." He leaned forward. "But you. They trust you. You can get information from these people. I'd make them suspicious if I started asking them if they saw this or heard this. People open up to you."

"I don't have to do anything illegal or anything that requires me to wear a gun, do I?" A gun would be neat, but I haven't fired one since my eleventh birthday.

"I'm not making you my deputy, for Christ's sake. Just listen. Just ask questions. Become that fact-finding journalist you use to be in High School."

Use to be? Not exactly the best way to ask me for assistance. A small town paper had the same duties and responsibilities as a metropolitan paper whether it's fact-finding or not. High School was years ago and fuck him if he didn't think I still had the same skills. I ran the paper in this damn town; who else would be qualified?

I took a breath and remembered that Bobby didn't know my history with my previous paper. He tried to give me a compliment and I was utterly shocked. Actually, the past twenty minutes had me shocked. Bobby reached out to me for help. Wait until

—naked Maggie mounting me and thrusting—

Maggie found out. Maggie's big-time jock couldn't solve The Case of the Mysterious Body without the nerd.

"All right. But keep me informed of anything you find out," I requested.

"I will."

On my way out, Gina stopped me. "Are you going to help him?" she asked.

"Yeah," I said. "Might as well. Don't have any other story to put in the paper right now."

She smiled. "I knew you'd come through."

"Bye."

I strolled back down to Main Street and headed back to my office for the third time today. Maybe I could get some things done before the whole sky came crashing down.

6

But first, I was hungry. I realized I hadn't eaten since my bologna and cheese sandwich from last night. *Betty's Grubs* sounded good.

The thin *ding* announced my arrival and I got a few waves from the local farmers. No '*Hey, Norm!*' but recognition was fun sometimes.

This was a typical classic diner. Each table had a checkerboard tablecloth and standard-issue restaurant chrome napkin dispensers and salt and pepper shakers. The paper placemats contained advertisements of local businesses that paid $25 per space. Al's Auto was on there as well as the *Ilton Gazette*. The place held around 125 people—as indicated by the Occupancy certificate—but only ten were in here now, including me, Betty and Kara.

Betty employed two waitresses and Kara was one of them. She was eighteen and worked a lot of nights during school. Since graduating early this October, Kara found herself also working days, until her winter session started at college. Right now, she filled ketchup bottles and she bent forward to put it back. Her short skirt hiked up and I saw a good portion of the back of her thighs. Smooth, bronze, nice. And if she would lean in a little more, I could probably catch a glimpse of her underwear. She sadly didn't need to lean and stood straight again and I was disappointed.

"Hey there, perv." Betty had snuck up on me. She smiled. "Just yourself?"

I nodded.

"Stay away from her, she's pure," Betty joked.

"No eighteen-year-old is pure," I said.

Betty pointed to a seat. "Sit your ass down." She pulled out her pen and pad. "Whatcha going to have today?"

"Burger and a couple of dills."

She didn't write it down. "Patty, two sticks," I heard her scream to her cook.

The clock on the wall read 1:30. I wouldn't get everything done by two like I hoped, but it would get done. Then, e-mail the stuff off to the printers and let everything ride. It's too bad I couldn't get any of the story from today in this week's edition. Start hooking those readers early and get it published like a serial story. Get Joe those ad sales.

I smelled the hamburger cooking when Alan, the auto shop owner who worried his ads failed, rushed through the door. He frantically shoved his way through the tables and everyone looked up.

"Somebody call an ambulance! Noogan's having a heart attack!" he yelled.

Kara dashed to the phone on the counter and dialed what I assumed was 911.

"Where is he?" I asked, standing.

"In the street. In the middle of the fucking street," Alan replied.

How could he leave him in the middle of the street? I sprinted to the door and glanced up and down the street. I missed him at first, and then saw a staggering man rolling along a parallel-parked car.

Noogan. And he didn't look good at all.

I ran to him and knelt by his side.

"Noogan! What's up old buddy?" I got a hand behind his back and propped him up. "We got an ambulance coming."

He nodded and then coughed. A bloody, gooey blob of phlegm ejected from his mouth and landed on my shoe. The skin on his face turned from a lush pink to an extremely pale white. I watched the iris of his eyes expand and contract as he tried to peer into my own eyes. Once, they rolled into the back of his head. He caught himself and with a little bit of energy, then grabbed a fistful of my shirt and dragged me closer.

"She screamed..." he muttered, trailing off.

"Who screamed?"

"*Her...*"

"Your daughter?" Nancy was a few years older than me and had moved back here from Las Vegas to take care of her dad. I wasn't sure, but I think she left behind a husband and a son. "Did Nancy scream?"

Noogan shook his head.

"Don't do too much. Let's wait for the paramedics."

"Iiiiit's tooooo...laaaate." Each word was forcefully stretched. It hurt him to speak, but he looked like he had to say it. "She screamed my death."

"Who did, Noogan? Who?"

"Reeeed, haaair...pretty..."

His fist relaxed and the arm fell to the street. His eyes stared into mine for a moment before his head flopped to the side and Noogan was no more.

I checked for a pulse and found none.

I leaned against the car and waited for the ambulance to arrive.

7

A screaming woman with red hair.

He couldn't mean the same one I saw at the creek. The coincidence was too much a coincidence. Maybe he saw a dream and it got to him. Much like a person with a queasy stomach had a hard time with boat rides. They may not puke on the first couple of trips, but eventually they would let it all fly.

I watched the ambulance ease away. No lights.

Betty put an arm around me.

"You okay?" she asked.

"Yeah. He was really disoriented."

"It's the Alzheimers."

I didn't know Noogan had Alzheimers. "Did anybody else know?"

"Him. Me. Maybe Miss Molly."

My curiosity perked. "Why would Miss Molly know?"

She smirked. "Come on. You know about them."

"I'm afraid I don't."

"He was probably over there right before he showed up here." She looked back at the restaurant. "Well, everybody seems to be parading inside. I better get back."

"Were they close friends?" I asked as she walked away.

"Close enough to share a bed." She laughed. "I can't believe you didn't know. Maybe we ought to replace you as the editor."

"Maybe we ought to build a second restaurant for competition," I said. "One with good food."

She laughed and waved me off.

Well, fuck me. Miss Molly.

Miss Molly lived on the Ritzy side of Ilton—if there was a side of Ilton called Ritzy with a population of 1100—where the two-story houses sported fenced-in backyards. *Whoopdeedoo.* The only advantage to living on that side was you had your mail early because the mailman started there. Miss Molly had lived here all her life. She worked as a secretary at the school and when she retired, she got a job as the park coordinator for the summer. I didn't know how many "Lock-Ins"—occasionally called Sock Hops by older parents—she's arranged for the town kids.

Her house was white the green shutters. The porch ran the entire front side of the house and on the left was a cellar entrance. Potted flowers sat on the steps and along the path to the sidewalk and in between each equidistant pot were solar lights. I caught their dim orange glow in the afternoon sun. I saw some gardening gloves and a pair of shears near one pot of flowers being replanted.

I knocked on the door. A few minutes later I heard a gate slam shut. Soon, Miss Molly emerged around the corner, shutting off a cordless phone. Tears had begun to dry on her face and she had a difficult time holding the phone. Her hands shook horribly as the phone fell to the ground. I dashed and picked it up, then handed it back to her. She took it, her hands still shaking. In her other hand, she held a small tape recorder—an instrument I was familiar with—and I heard it click. She lowered her hands.

"Oh my God," she murmured.

"Miss Molly?" I called out.

She looked up, startled. "Oh! Hi Grant."

"Sorry to scare you."

"I just got off the phone with Betty…"

"I'm sorry."

"It's crazy. He just left here thirty minutes prior."

I nodded. "I know. How did he seem when he left?"

"Fine, I think. We drank some lemonade and he was getting tired." She got lost in a recent memory. "He stayed the whole morning and wanted to go home and take a nap before we went to Chicago."

"What was in Chicago?"

"We were going to see *Wicked*."

"Good musical."

"Yeah." She sat on the steps.

"Can I ask you a strange question?"

"Sure."

"How did you two get together? I thought you pressed charges against him for running over your cat?" I asked. I hoped talking about Noogan would prime her up for my ultimate questions.

She laughed, her voice as shaky as her hands. "That's what brought us together. He came over to apologize after Chief Hamilton released him. I'm an old fashioned gal and was impressed with that. It takes a man to apologize. We talked and immediately became friends." When she said 'friends' her eyes lowered and her demeanor quickly dropped.

The relationship made sense. They're old, probably lonely. Why wouldn't they hit it off?

Now for the big question. "Let me ask you another strange question: right before he left, did you hear anything weird?"

Miss Molly thought for a second. "No. I don't think so."

"More specifically, a woman's scream." I sincerely hoped she didn't think I was being dirty or insinuated anything about their sex life—if one existed.

She thought again, but shook her head. "I'm sure I would have heard that."

"What did he do right before he left?"

"Well, he went into the cellar and was going to bring a bottle of my wine home to chill." She pointed to the cellar door.

"Can I go in there?"

"Why do you want to know so much?"

I should tell her. "He said he saw a red-haired woman and that he heard her scream."

"He didn't mention anything to me. He left right when he came out." She stood. "I'm going to finish my flowers. I don't want to think about it right now. Go ahead, it's unlocked."

"Thanks." I stopped. "What's with the tape recorder?"

"What—?" She turned her palm out and I saw the beige recorder nearly fall from her hand. "Oh this? I almost forgot. I use it to help me remember things…appointments, things I must do—you know—that old stuff."

I nodded. "Yup, I see."

Miss Molly just nodded.

"I'm sorry about Noonan. I know that you guys must have been close."

"Thanks," she said. "We were. This is just so…so, I don't know…"

She started to cry. How do you comfort an old lady? I smiled; that was rude of me to even think. I hope she didn't see me smiling. *Fuck*, I should just get out of here before I was a bigger ass.

"Tragic, Miss Molly," I said. She gave me a feeble smile. "Do you need anything?"

"No. I'm going to just work in the garden. Keep my mind off of it until I have to."

"I understand. Is it still okay if I check out the cellar?" I asked.

"It's fine."

"Okay. Just let me know if you need anything and I don't just mean now. You know where you can get a hold of me."

"Yes, thank you Grant. I appreciate that."

She disappeared around side of the house.

9

Instead of a handle, a frayed rope dangled from a hole where a handle use to be. The door opened surprisingly easy. A blast of cool air met me as I entered.

As the door shut, I saw a hanging bulb in the diminishing light. I tugged the string and a low-watt bulb threw soft yellow light about the room.

The cellar measured about twenty feet long and about seven feet wide and the ceiling rose a few inches above my head. I noticed a few water spots on the cement walls where leaks had started to occur. A damp odor filled my nostrils, but the cellar was very clean.

On the facing wall and halfway down the side walls in an encompassing "U" shape" were racks and racks of wine bottles. Just one layer deep from the floor to the ceiling. I estimated about 300 bottles. They stood straight up so that six bottles could fit vertically. The labels were meticulously aligned outward and all the bottles were unopened.

All except one.

I saw the glare at the end of the cellar. As I stepped closer, glass shards sparkled in the light. A broken bottle. *Noogan had the dropsies.*

Halfway down, I stopped.

The room was unusually cold now. Below freezing, if I had to guess the temperature. Just like that, room temperature to freezing. I touched the cement blocks. They were fine. It was just the air.

Even closer to the broken bottle, the air was barely tolerable. Who knew I needed a parka to check this cellar out. I reached the glass and knelt down. I picked up the still-intact label: *Gallo, 1946.* I knew jack crap about wine. It was old, so this must have been primo wine.

I dipped my finger in the spill and dabbed it on my tongue. Wine was wine in my opinion: strong alcohol smell and weak in the effects. I preferred the harder stuff. The manly stuff like straight vodka or whiskey. This wine shit was for prisses and old people. *But a glass of wine a day keeps the heart disease away.* True, but a glass of beer didn't make you queer.

"What happened down her Noogan?" I asked the room.

Something scraped the wall and I shot my head up. Nothing.

Then, the hanging light swung, bouncing the light from wall to wall, brushing the floor with circles. It arced like that for a few moments, then eased into a pendulum motion. I walked under the light and stopped it myself.

I quickly looked around, but it was just me. *Maybe Miss Molly killed him and had her way with him and now she wants you. She's going to lock you in here. Then while you nod off to sleep, she'll sneak in here and pull your pants down and rape you incessantly until you bleed and plead to die.*

—if it was Kara, no problem. Kara can rape—

The cellar door whipped open. Miss Molly stood there.

—it's time for the raping—

"Grant?"

I stepped into the light. "Yeah?"

"I heard something crash. You okay?" It was Miss Molly.

"Fine. Fine. Nothing crashed in here. At least not now. I found a broken bottle in the back. Noogan must have dropped it."

"Oh." Obviously, she didn't much care.

"You want me to clean it up?" I offered.

"I'll get it. I probably won't drink much wine anymore."

I understood. Hell, I wouldn't even want to go in that place. "Thanks for letting me go in there. If you happened to recall any strange sounds, call me, okay?"

"Okay." A half-hearted okay, but I wasn't going to press her anymore.

I left her as she gazed into the cellar. *Get away from there Miss Molly. Noogan's screaming red-headed woman will get you to.*

10

Maggie stopped me as I entered the office.

"Hamilton called. He wants to talk to you as soon as you get in," she said.

Couldn't the boy just leave me alone for one hour? "Thanks," I said. "After I talk to him, I'm going to go home. Can you finish up with the printers? Everything's almost done."

"Sure," she said. "You coming back?"

I trusted her with the printers. She had a great eye for layout and I've let her control the reigns on more than one occasion.

"I don't think so. I'm exhausted today for some reason."

"Some reason? I think you know the reason. You want to share it with the rest of the class?"

Joe and Pete looked up from what they were working on.

"Noogan died," I said, hoping that would delay the vultures.

"That's it?"

"That's it."

"Mmm-hmm." What the fuck? Had she been hanging out with Hamilton? Wait, she probably had been.

I retreated to my office and dialed Bobby.

"Bobby, it's Grant."

"Hey. We've ID'd the body."

That's interesting news. "And…"

"She's local."

"Okay, then why didn't we recognize her?"

He paused. "She's hasn't been local in over thirty years."

"She got out of town to escape its doldrums. Big deal."

"No," Bobby said, his voice shaking, "she's been *dead* for over thirty years. She's Noogan's grandmother."

"What?"

"She's Noogan's grandmother." He enunciated each syllable—which he didn't need to do because I heard him clearly the first time.

"Right. And I'm the Pope with a Vegas show. How the fuck does a body show up after being dead for thirty years? Wouldn't it decompose?"

"You would think. Maybe someone was keeping it on ice, or it was kept in a cool place. Sounds far-fetched, but possible."

I shook my head. "More far-fetched than possible."

"Just thought you'd like to know. Bye."

I hung up the phone in disbelief. What the hell was going on here? First this woman—who apparently was Noogan's grandmother—showed up, and then Noogan had a heart attack hours after. He claimed to have seen a screaming red-haired woman which described the same ghostly woman I saw. Only my lady didn't scream.

Somebody was playing a psychotic trick on us and it's turned annoyingly deadly. Sounded like some tagline for movie. *He was wronged and now, five years later, a trick to teach them all a lesson turns evil.* Wes Craven could direct and get all the stars of *Scream* back for one more go.

Something crazy was going on in Ilton. Someone needed to make nice.

For me, it was time for a nap.

CHAPTER THREE

1

Even though I trusted Maggie to take care of everything, I still worried as I walked through my apartment door. I threw my briefcase, keys and wallet on the wall table. I strolled by the kitchen, thinking I should grab a bite to eat because I might sleep through dinner and possibly beyond that. Nah. Vegging in front of the TV appealed to me more.

For an apartment, the front hallway stretched forever. I took a piss, then slammed my ass on the sofa and turned on the TV. I randomly selected a channel which happened to be The Movie Channel. *The French Connection* played and I saw it was halfway over. This cop drama was one of my favorite movies of all time and whenever it was on, I am able to watch it no matter what scene I came to. In the current scene Gene Hackman caught the sniper on his apartment and chased him down. That scene lasted for over 15 minutes. I'd probably be asleep by the end of it.

Something rattled behind me. I jumped up and waited.

Then, in the hallway, some kind of metal scrapped against wood. And it's digging deep.

I crept to the hallway and peeked out. Whatever it was, I caught the tail end of it whisking into the kitchen. There, silverware clattered against each other and pots and pans rang like bells. I tip-toed down the entrance hall. God, this hallway was fucking long.

The noise continued until I reached the kitchen doorway. At that moment, the strange sound abruptly stopped. I waited some more, each second ticking away like an hour. Whoever went in there would have to leave this way.

This is like some cliché horror movie. You hear sounds and you have to check it out. Walk slowly so the Evil Stuff has a chance to get you. And mind you, the Evil Stuff will always get you. You can try to run, you can try to hide, but Evil Stuff will win the fight.

I opened my eyes. Shit, I couldn't believe I had them closed in the first place.

A door slammed. My eyes lifted to the ceiling. I stood directly underneath my bedroom and I was positive the noise came from there.

No more cautiousness. I sprinted to my bedroom and flipped open the door. It was pretty smooth, if I do say so. I popped through the door just as the door swung completely open and hit the wall.

Nothing.

The room was freezing. Just like the cellar, except my entire bedroom was Antarctica.

The bedroom was not completely airtight, but a hole the size of a car could only create a draft like this. I took a couple steps inside. When I did, a breeze brushed the back of my neck.

Then I heard the door clap shut.

I'm in a bad B-horror movie! I screamed to myself. I shook my head and chuckled. I didn't know what my mind is trying to pull, but it was getting out of hand.

For one, the ceiling fan was on. That's probably what caused all this cool air in here. I got on my tip-toes, reached up and snagged the ball of the chain.

That's when I noticed her.

The woman from the forest. The woman Noonan fretted about.

She hovered over me, pressed against the ceiling. Frighteningly enough, she looked ready to *pounce*. To pounce on me.

The fan's blades whooshed by on the low setting and I pulled the chain twice more and heard the motor go silent. Should I move? Should I turn the fan back on high hoping the wind will blow her out of my fucking bedroom? Should I scream like a girl—

Those were the worst choice of words I could have thought.

Softly at first, a guttural squeal hit my ears. If it was any other sound, I might not have been bothered, but this squeal was different.

Fear.

I plugged each ear with my index fingers, but I still heard the scream like I hadn't shut out my ears.

Then it got louder.

And more fear.

"*Stooopppp!*" I picked up the closest thing I could nab—my $3.99 alarm clock from Big Lots—and hurled it at her.

Useless.

The clock slapped into the ceiling and came crashing down in pieces and broke into more pieces when it hit the floor. The display blinked 12:00 for a moment then slowly went blank.

Then the woman floated down and angled herself until she was vertical. Once again, like this morning, standing in front of me.

And yet here I stood, entranced. Not captivated or mesmerized, but *entranced*. I couldn't tear my eyes away.

She looked at me, then backed herself to the window. After letting out one quick high-pitched shriek, she dissipated through the wall.

2

I had a headache, I realized, and made my way to the bathroom.

I rummaged through my medicine cabinet, knocking bottles into the sink and my container of Q-tips onto the floor. The earsticks scattered and I went still, taking a breath, hoping all this would calm down.

"Fuck..." But I had no enthusiasm to care.

I found some Bayer and dumped some pills into my hand. I would have taken whatever landed in my palm, but deep down I was grateful only 4 of the 800 milligram things were there.

After popping them into my mouth, I leaned down and slurped water directly from the faucet. *You'll get germs and diseases*, my mom said every time she caught me doing that. Well, fuck her right now: I have a throbbing headache, as if someone was guiding a dull saw around my hairline.

It was time to lie down.

3

Each tree I touched is wet and cold even though it is 90 degrees outside. I see my campsite, torn to shreds. Surrounding trees spotted with blood. Whose? I touch the blood...fresh. I could still see it dripping onto the ground.

"William!" A woman's shout.

I spin towards the direction it came from.

"William! No!"

I run. I run, scared, but knowing I should run.

"Stay away!" This time it is a man. "Stay away from her!"

My feet get heavy and I start to slow. What's happening? Am I in mud? No. Too much brush? No. My feet are simply getting heavy. I bear forward, but that doesn't help.

I hear more shouts both from the woman and the man and it sounds frantic. But if I'm to save them or help them I sure am taking my own fucking sweet time getting there.

Finally, I break through a thick line of trees, a barrier…

And I see my mother and father in a small circular clearing. My mother is cowering at the base of an evergreen tree while my father holds out a cross. From my vantage it is the cross given to him by my grandmother. It is the size of my forearm and made of pure mahogany…no fake stuff. A gold circle with a gold cross of its own is inlaid at the intersection. But why is it used—

I gaze to my left and see—

— I try to move, but I am planted. Why and how still a mystery—

a cloud of mist forming a cone and racing up to the sky. Then nothing.

My father drops his guard and rushes to my mother. He kneels and holds up her torso.

"You okay?" he asks.

She nods, but it's a weak nod. She's not okay.

I can move now and I run to their sides.

"What's wrong?" I ask.

They don't answer.

"What's wrong!!?" I ask again.

My father tries to lift her up.

"Don't," she says, "I can't feel anything in my body."

"Your legs? You can't move?" My father tries lifting her again.

"No. I can't feel anything inside *my body. I can't feel my heart beating." She leans back against the tree.*

My father slumps to the ground and takes my mother's hand. He's defeated.

"Dad! No! Get her to the hospital!"

I bend over and take my mom's...

—oh god please no, I need my mom—

and my hand slides right on through her body.

"No...mom..."

In the next second her eyes roll up and her chest stops moving.

My father knows and silently stands. He jabs his hands under my mother and lifts her up.

I cry.

I watch my father walk into the edge of the forest—

4

And I wake, sweating.

Crying and sweating.

What a dream. I sat up, squinting so my eyes could adjust from sleep. It took a minute, but soon I saw I was alone and I relaxed a bit.

I looked over to check the time and see that my clock was not there. My stomach dropped because I realized where it was. I glanced at the floor. Sure enough, the clock mocked me. *Haha fucker. You used me to defend yourself and now I'll never show you the time again. That's what you get.*

No, what I get was wondering what time it was.

I used the pillow to wipe the sweat from my forehead and back of my neck, then I got out of bed. I would have to take care of the mess later. Right now I needed something to drink.

Nothing hard. Just something to quench my dream-caused thirst.

5

I pulled a beer out and twisted off the top. The swig was heaven, like silk being draped over my esophagus.

The clock over the sink read 3:45.

"3:45? That's it?" I chugged the last of the beer and set the bottle on the counter.

My people know that when I say that I was going home for the afternoon on Tuesday, I didn't really mean it. Sometime later, they usually expected me to return before everyone went home for the day and today was no different. Maggie surely had everything to the printers by now. I think I just wanted to go to the paper and relax.

That's right: I was going to my job to relax.

I called Maggie and told her and she wasn't shocked I planned on coming back. She asked if there was anything I wanted her to do, but I said that everyone can go home. I wanted the office to myself.

6

I turned the last corner before the *Gazette's* building and saw it was blocked half way down. Most normal people would have yelled out a "Come on! Someone had better of died up there" and waited, but not me. I ran a newspaper. My brain kicked into investigative mode.

As I approached the blockade of police cars (two of Bobby's crew and two county cruisers) a fire engine, and an ambulance, I realized they were in front of Miss Molly's house. I raced closer and jumped out. I headed to the lawn.

Bobby must have seen me because he moved to intercept me.

"What's going on?" I asked him.

He looked back, then guided me back to my car. "Fuckin' county's here," he muttered. "Some asshole called county instead of me."

"That doesn't make him an ass—"

"Yes it does. *Their* fingers are going to be in it now." He sighed. "I didn't want that."

"Bobby why are they here?"

"Miss Molly."

"She okay?"

"No...she..." and he couldn't say it. A shake in his voice; a blubber. I watched his eyes well up. Any other time I'd be pressed to spew a quip which would spark some sarcastic comment from Bobby and we'd go toe to toe—or word for word—for a few minutes before getting irritated with each other. But now, I felt a little compassion for him.

"Is she dead?" I finally asked. I knew the answer already.

"Yes, she is."

"How?"

Again, he looked back. "No one knows," he said.

"Any clues at all? Come on Bobby, help me out here."

"Grant, settle down. I don't know anything and neither does county. We all just got here...well, county first of course."

I glanced behind him and saw a few county cops leaving the house. One shook his head, but not in disgust or fear or anything, but more like *I really don't have a clue.*

"Maybe I can take a look. Get an objective view—"

Bobby shook his head. "Not right now. Wait until later. I'll let you go in tonight."

"Sure."

"Just do me a favor and go. I'll call you when it's clear."

Was he going to really let me go in there? I had a slight distrust in him actually carrying out his promise. I'll see later I guess.

"Don't forget," I said.

He grunted—which I assumed was an 'okay'—and left, heading back towards the house.

7

The air was shut off when I walked through the *Gazette's* front door—and it was damn humid in here. I let the door shut behind me, then immediately went to the thermostat and clicked it down to 70 degrees. The air kicked on.

My office invited me. I had missed it all afternoon. I shut the door and everything went quiet. To me, this was solace.

What wasn't solace was the silver hairbrush sitting on my desk. The hair brush that Bobby showed me earlier today. The hair brush that now mocked me, grinning its evil *I've got you now* smile in case I would forget that a piece of evidence found near a body sat on my desk.

Calm down Grant. Just figure it out. Be a reporter, like in the old days.

The old days? Shit, that was only like 3 years ago. Surely I could remember how to investigate. Maybe becoming an editor *had* made me soft, like Bobby said.

—shut up shut up shut up concentrate—

First, how did the brush get here? That was the all-important question. Someone must have brought it over. So who? The office was usually locked when no one was inside and only Maggie and I had a key. Problem: Maggie had no idea about the brush or any of the "issues" of the past day. So she couldn't have done it.

Magic? The Great and Wonderful Appearing Hairbrush of the Grandmother Noonan? Not likely.

So the first question wasn't answered.

Then second: why was the brush here? Did Bobby feel a joke was in order? An unfunny tasteless joke that didn't make any sense? Why would he play the joke on me? Okay, that's probably a stupid question. Maybe this brush wasn't even here at all.

I closed my eyes then reopened them. Sure enough the brush was still here.

Still mocking.

I've got you now.

"Fuck you." Yeah that's it. Curse at the inanimate object. That's really editor-like.

But it did have me now because I couldn't explain how it got here or why it was here. And there was still the problem of when it got here, who it belonged to, where it had been before it was on my desk, but fuck the 5 W's and H. I couldn't answer the obvious questions so who the hell did I think I was to answer the other ones.

I should call Bobby and tell him the brush was here. Maybe after I get into Miss Molly's house and see what was going on there.

I grabbed some newspaper and used that to grasp the hairbrush. Then I unlocked my cabinet—which I only have the key to—and placed it far in the back. I shut the drawer and locked it.

Then I checked the cabinet again to make sure it was locked. I didn't want anyone to find this. No one really had any reason to be in this cabinet, but I guess I got a flash of OCD.

8

My desk phone rang.

"Who—" I picked it up. "Hello?"

"Get over here." It was Bobby. "It's clear."

CHAPTER FOUR

1

The brush occupied my mind on the way over. And well it should. Mostly I thought about whether I should mention the thing to Bobby. I knew I wouldn't, why kid myself? I should get rid of it, that's what I should do. Break it in half; take a hammer to it; or return to my campsite and ignite the fire again and toss the brush in until the silver turned to liquid metal and sizzled into oblivion.

As I approached Miss Molly's house, Bobby stood on the porch. This time though, he didn't come out to meet me. His scrunched face glared at me the entire time I walked to the house.

"Hey Bobby," I said.

"Hey," he grumbled.

I decided not to say anything about the brush. His demeanor decided that.

Bobby thrusted a walkie-talkie at me. "Here, take this," he said.

"What's this for?"

"In case I need to warn you."

"Warn me?" I chuckled. "Warn me from what?"

"If anyone is coming."

"You're insane—"

Bobby squeezed my hand around the radio. "Shut up and take it. County might come back."

"At this hour? I pretty much doubt it." I stuck the walkie in my pocket.

"Yeah at this hour…"

"Are we covert or what?"

"You got 10 minutes." Bobby's humor quickly vanished. "That's all. Just ten minutes."

"Fine." I surveyed the house, gazing at the six windows overlooking the street. "Where was she found?"

"Her bedroom. Second floor."

"Is that where she died?"

"I assume so. I'm not sure. I didn't get to go in the house once county got the investigation going."

I turned, ready to enter, and Bobby stopped me. "You'll need this. Don't turn the lights on."

He handed me a flashlight. I clicked it on. A bright, thin beam slapped Bobby in the face. A small gleam of satisfaction flowed through me.

He shielded his eyes in surprise. "Turn that fucking thing off! Not out here! You stupid or something…*editor*?"

Prick.

I walked through the door and shut it as quickly as I could to give myself the illusion Bobby wasn't out there. I didn't know how productive I'd be knowing he was out there wondering what I was doing in here. But I knew he was. Out of sight, out of mind…for now.

The house smelled like my grandmother's house. A little musty and old. The air was slightly humid, so the musty smell just kind of hung there, never getting stronger but never going away either.

My eyes adjusted a little, but I still had trouble seeing. I made out a small foyer table with outlines of flowers—tulips maybe—and a coat rack with a trench coat on it. I turned on the flashlight and saw that the flowers were tulips and the coat wasn't a trench coat, but a blue Peacoat, with the big buttons, like the sailors wear. Not much else was in here.

The hallway extended the length of the house and at the end was the kitchen. I took a few steps inside the yellow décor and saw the living room on my right. A corner couch; a few guest chairs; and a curio cabinet full of little figurines. I estimated about a hundred or so. They looked in pristine condition.

The living room went off to the left about ten feet where a large dining table sat bare. Behind it, a chest with a hutch full of bright white china. Also well taken care of. A grandfather clock stood behind me, its pendulum still at some undeterminable time with no one to wind the gears. I looked at the clock's hands: they were stuck on 6:49.

I slipped out my walkie. "Bobby, what time did Miss Molly die?" I released the button and it *Chhhhhked*.

A click returned. "The walkie is only for me to use." A pause, and then, "A little before 7 p.m."

Other than the grandfather clock, nothing else interested me here.

I went through the alternative entrance to the kitchen through the living room. Fridge, stove, a breakfast nook, large counter space. I dreamt of having that kind of counter space. I wondered if this was a remodeled kitchen or if this was how she got it when the house was bought. I made a mental note: find out when the house went to market.

Nothing seemed out of ordinary here.

Back into the hallway from the opposite end of the foyer, a small hallway jutted to my right. I followed it. A bathroom stood on my left. I shone the light in there. The scent of Lysol lingered. Clean. The medicine cabinet had been cleared at some point. County? In the tub was a clump of dark hair living on the drain. County forgot to take that.

I left the bathroom and followed the hallway to the right. A weirdly laid out first floor; the only thing down at this end was a bedroom.

I waved the light through. This probably became a guest room when company arrived. It had a double-sized bed, one chest of drawers and a small tube TV.

So far my hunt was disappointing.

But what's to be disappointed about when nothing exciting happened on the first floor anyway? It was the second floor that saw all the action.

My walkie crackled.

"Hurry up in there," gasped Bobby.

I don't know what his deal was. No one had planned to come to this house at this time of night. They'd be seriously fucked in the head to do that. Who liked to visit the house of someone that recently died in it? Weirdos, that's for sure.

Like me.

Shit, *I'm* the weirdo.

"I just got to check upstairs, then I'm out," I responded. *Chhhk.* When he didn't answer, I put the walkie back in my pocket and went to the front door, where I saw stairs.

I paused at the foot of the stairs.

Wasn't it always the trip upstairs that screwed you over? You knew better not to go up there, but for some messed up reason, you concluded that hey, it was probably safe. Don't worry about the murderer or possible psychopath waiting to decapitate you.

"Yeah, it's probably safe," I said, smirking.

The first step creaked when I put my weight on it. Great, a creaking step. I envisioned an axe murder waiting at the top to swing an oversized axe at my head, quipping "You don't have a good head about ya, do ya."

I smiled. I needed to stop scaring myself.

Instead of trudging up the stairs, I took them two at a time and paused at the top. No axe murderer here.

I arced the flashlight through the hall. Two doors on the right and three on the left, with large family portraits lining the wall. My flashlight hit a medium-sized picture at the far end and I'll be damned if it wasn't Old Man Noonan.

Get 'em Noonan! How many years were they together? Must have been a lot of years since Noonan had his own spot on the wall.

Other pictures included actual family. Grandchildren, daughters, sons, nephews, nieces. Some frames had multiple pictures in them. Probably all from one family or one side of the family. Names were typed under them, but I had Bobby blowing my ass around because he was nervous about someone stopping by. No time to get to know Miss Molly's family.

The first room seemed to be a storage room. There was a small bed in there, but it was piled with scrapbooking materials. On the floor were small storage books with what looked like photographs. I flipped one of the lids open and saw faded, orange-color pictures with people dressed in fancy duds and sporting handlebar mustaches. Early 1900's no doubt. I replaced the lid and went into the room across the hall.

An office or study of some sort. One wall held hundreds of books. Many were hardbound, but a few glass shelves appeared devoted to paperbacks. A reading chair and large lamp sat in one corner and a waist-high sized globe gazed at me from the opposite corner, with Europe shouting a little hello. A desk with computer and old CRT monitor stood near the door. The computer was currently off and the keyboard shelf pushed in.

SCRRRREEEEEEEEEEE!!!

What the hell was that? It came from across the hall.

SCREEEEE!!

A short one, but still piercing. My ears throbbed for a moment after.

I turned my flashlight off and snuck to the shut door. Did it have to be shut? Did I shut it?

My hand went to the doorknob. I jumped back. I looked at my palm. It already started turning red.

I tapped the doorknob with my fingers. Freezing. My eyes finally adjusted from shutting off my flashlight and I saw little frost pimples forming on the brass handle. I put my hand under the hem of my shirt and used the fabric as a barrier to grab the handle. I slowly turned the doorknob and pushed the door open.

And there she was.

Again.

She floated over the bed, but this time her back was to me. She seemed to peer out the window.

I pulled out the walkie-talkie. Before I could push the button to call Bobby—

SCCCCRRRRREEEEEEEEEEEEEEEEEEEEEEEE!

Fuck!

I dropped to my knees and let the radio fall to the floor. I clapped my palms over my ears to shut out the sound, but like before it was futile.

Finally, the screeching stopped.

Then, over the walkie, "What in the living fuck was that?" Since Bobby heard it, I wondered how many neighbors would start getting curious. Would we see lights pop on down the block because of the noise?

I looked down. The walkie had landed on the button side, pressing it down.

"Grant?"

I lifted the walkie to my mouth. "Yeah..."

"What the hell was that screaming?"

"I don't know."

"Did you hear it?"

"Yes."

"You see anything?"

I stared at the woman. She still looked out the window.

"No," I answered.

"Are you sure."

I paused.

"Yes," I finally said.

I turned the walkie off. No more interruptions.

Apparently the woman didn't notice me. I took one step forward and when she didn't acknowledge that movement, I crept to the window.

"What are you looking at?" I mumbled.

I followed her gaze.

Bobby sat in his squad car. I watched him messing with his walkie. He tapped it against the steering wheel. I checked the woman's eyes. She looked higher, over Bobby's car. There was one light on down the whole street.

It was Betty's house. Now why was she looking at Betty's house?

I turned back to her and she then lowered her head so she was looking at me. *SHREEEEEEE!* It was softer, as if only meant for me.

Betty's house went dark and Bobby talked on his walkie, trying to reach me. And when I turned back and she was gone.

A thin mist spiraled towards the ceiling and disappeared within seconds.

4

As I emerged from the house, Bobby jumped out of his car and sprinted to me.

"What took you so long and did you hear that squeal?" He was out of breath. So much for that academy training. Being a Police Chief of a small town made you flabby, I guessed.

"There are a lot of rooms in that house."

"What about the sound?"

"Sound? It's all quiet in there."

"No, there was a high-pitched scream."

Hiding the fact I had the brush in my possession and lying to the Police Chief, I believed I was starting a string of bad behavior. Hell, I should just start my run of bank robberies now.

"Bobby, I didn't hear a thing." I looked him in the eye. Isn't that what professional liars did?

"You said you did."

"Did I? I may have heard the walkie-talkie go off or squeal or something."

"Mmm-hmm."

"I didn't see anything either." Bobby wasn't convinced; I wasn't really trying either. I watched his eyes dart back and forth from me to the house and back again. I bet he wanted to have a look for himself.

"Listen," I said, "You might just need to go home and get some sleep. You've had a long day. Three deaths and county coming in and taking over: that would be stressful for anyone."

Bobby relaxed a little.

"It's no wonder you're hearing things," I added.

He sunk his head. "Yeah, you're right I guess. I am tired."

"Go home and rest. Pick up the rest of the trails tomorrow."

I couldn't believe I actually gave this asshole some sincere advice. I secretly hoped that he would go in there and see the thing, hear her screams, and simply just keel over. Then she would

—feast on his body on his mind on his soul I think his soul tastes like dirt—

"I will. Thanks Grant."

Before I could say anything else, Bobby hopped in his car and slumped down. He *was* tired. He started his car, gave one look back at the house, then pulled away.

And it was silent. My watch read 2:30 a.m. Where the fuck did the time go? Surely I wasn't in the house for 3 hours.

When Bobby was completely out of sight, I turned around and went back to the house.

5

I bypassed the first floor and immediately headed upstairs. Everything still appeared in order as I had seen it earlier. I *must* have missed something. Something small or odd that I really didn't know was odd or out of place or related to Miss Molly's death.

The picture of Noonan actually creeped me out, when I actually got a good look at it, sending small pings of shivers down my back. A dead old lady's house and her dead lover's picture hung just feet from me.

I checked the study once more, this time using my flashlight to reach the harder-to-see areas: under the reading chair, under the desk, around the globe. Still, nothing. What did a guy have to do to find something here?

Back to the bedroom.

I swept the light across the room and initially saw nothing. Then I reverted to my original tactic of checking the out of the way places. Under the dresser, under the TV stand, under the bed—

What was that?

Something gleamed against the light as the beam hit it. A silver object.

I got on my hands and knees and scooted to the bed. I shone the light under there again and saw a tape recorder lying randomly on the floor, as if thrown there. I latched onto it and brought it into the open.

This was the same tape recorder the Miss Molly had earlier. She had died in here. I wonder—

I rewound the tape a little bit and pressed play.

I heard a car drive by and outside air pushing into the microphone. *"Oh this! I almost forgot. I use it to help me remember things...appointments, things I must do, you know that old stuff,"* I heard Miss Molly say.

Then I heard me say, *"Yup, I got ya."*

That was earlier today. Strange hearing her voice.

The recording clicked off. Then a tight squeak. Then recording again.

"Who are you?" A pause. *"How did you get in here?"* Another pause.

Then a loud piercing scream gurgled distortedly on the tape. The microphone still handled the noise.

"Oh my God—"

Then silence.

"Where did you go…?"

The doorbell rang on the tape. Then I heard some scratching as the tape recorder was probably placed in a pocket. The sounds became muffled after that.

Miss Molly started walking. She opened the door.

"Oh, hi again."

Again?

A man answered, but I couldn't make him out.

"Come in."

Who can come in?

"Would you like something to drink? I have an amazing story to tell you. It just happened."

The man answered, still inaudible.

"What are you doing?"

Who is this? And what are they doing?

Panicked running—up stairs?—then a door slammed shut. More scratching and then a thud. She must have thrown the recorder under the bed at this point.

"What is that? What are you DOING!?" Pause. *"Grant! Stay away!"*

Something cracked: a bone sound. The voice activated control shut the machine off and all was quiet.

But me? I was here earlier?

I ran through my day: campsite, called Hamilton, dealt with Hamilton, witnessed Noonan die, spoke with Miss Molly, came to her wine cellar, left, napped—nothing made sense. I had no problem admitting I talked to Miss Molly today, but that was for about, what, ten minutes at most?

More disturbing though:

I killed Miss Molly.

CHAPTER FIVE

1

I sped home. It took me less than a minute to get there. I quickly sprinted to my apartment, nervous sweat soaking my face. I was also breathing nervously and couldn't catch my breath as I put my hands on my knees and doubled over by the front door. The world around me looked far away, as if escaping the horrors of my mind, escaping the fact that I had undeniable proof I killed Miss Molly. My knees screamed betrayal and I dropped to the floor; two small jolts of pain ripped around my legs.

Then a thick stream of puke ejected from my mouth. My stomach heaved, shuddering until everything was out that my body thought would be enough.

I stepped inside my apartment and felt sick again. This time I was able to hold down the muscle that wanted to push the puke up.

There was no fucking way I killed Miss Molly. But there it was on the tape. My name clear as day coming out of Miss Molly's mouth.

No, it couldn't have been me. I was at the office all evening and at my apartment earlier that day.

That woman. That woman had something to do with this. That fucking screaming bitch who floated, appearing everywhere I do. I didn't have anything to do with anything.

I went into the kitchen and splashed cold water on my face. I needed to sleep. Just like Bobby, I had a long day. That's it. Sleep.

The bed welcomed me. Just lie down, go to sleep and tomorrow morning everything will be just fine. One long daydream, that's all this was. I took my shirt off, then removed my pants and threw them in the corner. When they hit the wall, I heard a loud *THUD!*

Shit. The tape recorder.

I reluctantly took it out of the pant's pocket and stared at it. Play it? Or just forget about it? I definitely heard my name on the tape, but did I need to hear it again or see this damned thing again?

No.

For now, I lifted up my mattresses with one hand and tossed the recorder underneath.

I pulled back the sheets and slipped in. Tomorrow everything will be over. No tape recorder, no dead Miss Molly. Hell, Old Man Noonan will be alive I bet.

I drifted…

2

Five years after my mother died, my father has turned to liquid. Liquid alcohol. Drinking every day. Hard stuff, wine coolers, beer. Anything that could take the edge off of the memory.

I understood none of it. I only understood that my mother had been gone for five years and my father became more distant by the day, the week, the year. Was there anything I could do about it? Nothing.

One morning in October, we see her again. The woman that appeared when my mother died. The scream doesn't wake me, just her presence.

My dad is up first, already holding a small glass of amber liquid in his right hand. He stands, staring at her. She slightly floats in the living room, barely inches above the floor. If she wasn't pale or white, she could actually pass for someone alive.

"Dad," I say.

He doesn't move.

"Dad," I say again. "Dad, what are you doing?"

He shuffles back slightly, coming out of his trance for a moment. "Huh," he murmurs.

"Let's get out of here," I say.

"She hasn't screamed yet," is all he says. "She will, I just know it."

"Dad? What do you mean?"

The woman floats towards my dad.

I grab my dad's hand and pull him out of the living room.

"She'll always be here," he says menacingly. The glass slips from his hand. Shards and liquor splash everywhere. On a second look, I notice a couple drops of red. I turn my dad's hand over and see some cuts. The blood drips out, creating small kaleidoscopic dots in the mess on the floor.

"We need to clean that up." I say.

He looks at the glass and booze. "Okay." He kneels down, but I pull him back up.

"No, your cuts."

His eyes dart back into the living room. The woman jerks around, gawking at us. Waiting for our next move? Waiting to scream again? Waiting for more blood? Do I want to know?

I drag my dad upstairs and into the bathroom and shut the door.

"She won't get us in here." He looks at me. Neither of us feels convinced at his statement.

With the cold water on, I stick my dad's bleeding hand under the water until the blood washes away and the flow ceases enough to put some gauze on the wounds.

I dry the hand off and lay the gauze over the cuts. This shouldn't be happening. He is supposed to be treating any hurts I get. Sons should not be tending to their fathers.

A tear travels down my cheek.

My father sees it I think. He uses his other hand to wipe it free from my face.

"I'm going to die," he says.

So matter-of-fact I believe him.

"It's her," he says.

"What's her?" I wrap his hand with tape as best I could.

"I'm going to die," he says again.

"Quit saying that! You're not going to die!" I throw the metal container of tape against the bathroom door. My dad shrinks against the toilet.

Meekly, he says, "I am."

"I won't let you." Just a little reassurance. He'll be fine.

"You won't let me, but you can't stop her." He stands and leaves me in the bathroom to fear his last statement.

I believe him.

3

I woke from the dream delirious, unsure of where I was or when it was.

4:06 a.m.

Why was I having those dreams? They didn't start until *she* arrived. I mean, it's been a while since my parents died: what was the purpose of me dreaming about it now? I've grieved. I grieved soon after and for some time after. Did my subconscious find it necessary to send me signals to grieve again? I didn't understand any of this shit.

Just fucking weird was what it was.

She came, three people died and I started having dreams about my mom and dad.

I lied in bed for some time, pushing down the part of me that wanted to go to sleep because I knew what thoughts and dreams would swirl in my brain. I tried; I couldn't fight it. My body relaxed and slowly, my mind drifted off.

I quickly found myself with my dad again…

4

The next morning I hear my dad in the kitchen clanging pans and laying out dishes. Things must be better, I thought.

Still groggy, I trudge downstairs. He is making breakfast. I smell the wonderful aroma of bacon, eggs, and toast.

"Morning dad," I say.

"Morning." Monotone. He still remains a little sleepy himself.

He turns around and opens the fridge. He is in there for a few minutes, searching for something.

"Shit," he mumbles.

"What's wrong?"

"No cheese."

"It's okay. I don't want cheese."

He shuts the fridge door. "I do. I'm going to run to the store."

"Really? But the food. It's almost done."

"Eggs are no good without cheese."

"They're just eggs."

He stops and looks at me. "I want cheese," he says.

"Okay, okay."

He grabs his car keys from the hook by the back door. The door clicks shut. Moments later the car starts and I hear the gravel crunch as he leaves the driveway.

Had I known it would also be the time my dad would leave this Earth, I would have fought a little harder to get him to stay home. I should have tried screaming, yelling or throwing a tantrum.

But would it have made a difference? Would he have died anyway at some point? I don't know. Maybe. I had watched my mom die. I guess in some morbid way I was glad I didn't get to see my other parent die.

It is on the way back from the grocery store. Another car T-boned my dad's car. My dad didn't wear his seat belt, which is odd for him; but regardless, he didn't wear it. The paramedics got to him quickly but they say he died about ten minutes after impact.

My neighbor takes me to "the scene." Mr. Underwood calls it "the scene." Like he is some detective. He is just my ride to "the scene."

I don't get there in time to see him alive. I get there in time to see him getting carried away on the stretcher with the sheet drawn up over his face.

Mr. Underwood draws me close. He keeps whispering "I'm so sorry, Grant. So sorry." But I barely hear him. Everything goes silent around me as I watch the ambulance drive away with no lights on.

"Let's go," Mr. Underwood says.

I catch a glimpse of a package on the sidewalk near the car. It gleams in the morning sun.

I break from Mr. Underwood's grasp and run to the package. It is a package of Kraft American Cheese. Still brand new and just from the store: little droplets of water connecting with the morning humidity run down the blue and red plastic. Thrown from the car, still fresh.

I pick it up and jam it in my pocket.

"Are you ready now?" Mr. Underwood asks.
I could only nod.

5

This time when I woke, the clock read 6:17 a.m. At least I got a couple more hours sleep. Something fell down my face. I wiped it with one of my fingers.

A tear.

My father died twice. Once in reality, once in my dream. But he said something in the dream.

"It's her," he had said. *"I'm going to die."* And, *"You can't stop her."*

I jumped out of bed.

"Shit!" I ran downstairs, threw on my shoes and sprinted to my car. I had to get to Betty's.

6

I didn't even shut the car off as I stopped in front of Betty's house. I hopped out and ran up to her house.

I knocked.

No answer. I knocked harder, my knuckles stinging from the wood.

"Betty?"

Still nothing.

I sidled to the closest window. A lace curtain blocked my view, but I could make out an active TV in her living room. I rapped on the window. The glass *TINGED*! Despite how loud that was, I still obtained no answer.

"Betty!"

I pushed against the locked door with my shoulder. The flimsy oak gave a little. I stepped back and put a little more force behind my surge and something splintered on the other side. Everyone on the block would hear that and come out of their houses and to watch me. I was a little embarrassed that I would actually have to break down Betty's door.

Taking a further step back, I pressed off my feet and launched myself at the door.

Lucky for me the door gave on that take and the door swung inward. I tumbled in and listened for a second as I crouched on my knees.

The TV rattled off some sitcom. Canned laughter, then more talking, then more canned laughter. Other than that, I heard nothing else.

I quietly shut the door and stood up.

"Betty? Are you here?"

Betty lived by herself, widowed 12 years ago. She never remarried and if you asked her, she would tell you, "I had the one love of my life for 31 years. There is no other for me. I just want friends now." Her husband Vernon died in the field, tilling his dirt. Heatstroke. But Betty was happy. You couldn't convince her otherwise. A smile always exhibited on her face and she had a handy joke if you needed one. Forget about the restaurant. *Betty's Grubs* was the greasy spoon that everyone in a hundred mile radius wanted to eat at.

I meandered my way around the furniture and followed the sound of the TV. The show had given way to a commercial. Somebody was selling car insurance. As I entered the TV room, an announcer relayed the effects of some drug called *Hertiva*, which I recalled had just been put on the market.

But the room was empty.

"Betty!" I screamed.

I headed towards the kitchen and I had to stop for a second. I saw thick-soled shoes protruding out into my view. That didn't sit well.

"Betty?"

But I knew. Deep in my soul I knew.

Betty was dead.

I calmly entered the kitchen. I was right.

Betty lied face down on the kitchen floor. One of her shoes hung half off her foot. The other shoe had been dragged through a pile of chocolate pudding. I knelt down and jabbed my finger in the pile of pudding. I tasted it. Chocolate pudding. The exact pudding at her restaurant. She must had been making some for the day.

I rounded the wooden kitchen island. Betty's bifocal glasses spilled to the side, smashed flat. In her right hand she held a wooden spoon, her grip still tight.

The only thing I could do was to call Bobby. I didn't know how happy he'd be since I had to call him at home.

He picked up on the first ring, though. "Bobby," I said. "You need to come to Betty's house."

"Why?" He yawned.

"She's dead."

"What?" A pause. "I'll be right there."

7

Bobby did get right here. Less than five minutes later, I heard his squad car, complete with sirens, screeching up alongside my car.

I met him at the door.

"What the fuck?" He asked.

When I realized he wasn't going to stop, I swung back to let him through.

"Where is it?" He spat out.

"It?"

"The body."

"Betty is *not* an it."

"Knock it off, Grant. Just show me."

I lead him through the TV room and into the kitchen.

He saw her there and shook his head. "Who the fuck did this? Who the fuck would do this to her? To *Betty*?" Bobby quickly surveyed the scene and looked like he made a few mental notes. He paused on the pudding.

"There's a fingerprint in there."

"I did that."

"You got shit for brains? Why would you touch that?"

"Just wanted to see—"

"Just wanted to see? See what? How good her fucking pudding was?" Bobby shook his head again. "I can't believe this Grant. I can't believe *you*."

"It's just pudding!" I yelled.

Just as he did at the campground, Bobby took a pen and knelt down. He used the pen to rotate Betty's head.

Bobby glimpsed at me in shock. "It's a crime scene, is what it is."

"How do you know?"

"The stab wounds."

I missed those. How could I have missed those? I stood next to Bobby.

Three gashes on her neck. Each one was about an inch or two. The first line started just below the jaw line and headed straight down her neck. The second started on the same side as the first and began where the base of her neck met the collarbone. The final gash, which probably was the only one really needed, cut right across her throat. It was as if the killer messed up the first two times or didn't really know how to properly slice a throat with the intent of death. The third gash went about three inches in length and appeared to be the deepest. How could I have not seen those earlier? Poor Betty. I guessed the only thing I touched was the pudding Bobby was having a hemorrhage over.

Chief Bobby Hamilton rose. "So why were you here?"

"Don't you need to call the coroner or something?" I smirked. "Or county?"

"Fuck county." He peered at me for a few second before asking his next question. "So why were you here? To get a jump on some of Betty's pudding?"

"I was driving by and didn't see Betty at the restaurant and got a little worried. She's usually there by 6 a.m."

"Mmm-hmm," was all Bobby said.

"What are you saying Bobby?"

"Chief Hamilton, please."

"*WHAT ARE YOU SAYING?*"

Bobby took out a notepad. "If I need to get a hold of you today, where can I reach you?"

Now I was in shock. "At my fucking office. Am I a suspect?"

"Right now, yes. I may have some more questions for you later. I need to look over the scene, so if you'll excuse me…" He took out his cell phone and dialed a number.

"Thanks a lot, *Chief Hamilton*," I murmured.

"Watch it Grant. We may know each other as residents of this town and former classmates, but I do NOT have to go easy on you or give you the benefit of the doubt."

"I guess you don't follow the innocent until proven guilty adage that everyone else does." Bobby and I were back to old times, except in more extreme circumstances than we ever had been.

Bobby snapped his cell phone shut.

"It's funny," he said, "that there have been three deaths in this town and one body found and you have been around all of them!"

"So I caused Noonan's heart attack?" I laughed. "Reality check, Chief: he was having the attack before I got there. And that body? It was already dead, you forget that?"

Bobby waited for me to continue. I knew he wanted me to say something about Miss Molly and Betty, but I had nothing for Betty. Miss Molly though—

"I was *not* there when Miss Molly died," I said.

"But you were there just a couple hours before, weren't you?" he countered.

"Yes, but to do a little investigation myself."

"Right. Because you're a detective."

"This is ridiculous." I headed for the door.

"You'll be at your office, right?"

I didn't answer. I just left. Because it *was* ridiculous.

8

So now I was a suspect. What did suspects do when they find out they were one? I assumed they just went about their day. So I would do the same, I supposed. I would go home, take a shower, get dressed, eat breakfast, and leave for work. That's what I would do.

And oh yeah, I would probably get a call from Chief Bobby Hamilton, who graduated 214th in the class out of 229. Perfect police material. The perfect crime fighter.

I got home, took a shower, quickly dressed, then ate some Raisin Bran.

I grabbed the set of keys from the key hook and when I went into the living room to find my wallet, I saw it.

The steak knife.

It rested on my couch. I closed my eyes to push the image away and when I opened my eyes, I noticed its dark brown handle staring at me, as if saying "*Hey, remember our exceptional embrace just hours ago? Remember how*

your hand made love to me as you jabbed me into Betty?
We enjoyed it, didn't we? A stabbing good time!"

Something red sat in little globs on the blade. I was afraid of what it might be. I imagined the worst possible thing it could be and when I walked over—

Shit, it was.

Blood.

I picked up the steak knife by the handle and a few more drops of blood fell on my couch.

Dammit. I ran to the kitchen and found two baggies big enough for the knife. I had to hide it. I could put it with the hairbrush.

The knife fit perfectly in the baggie. I was concerned about the blade cutting the plastic, so I put *that* baggie in the second one. That should be fine. Besides it was just going to sit in the drawer.

9

No one was at the office which was good. My heart continued to pound against my chest.

I unlocked the door and sauntered through the desks. I still half-expected somebody to either be sitting in here or busting through the door in a lucky attempt to expose me. I made it to my office in the clear and shut the door.

My breath finally relaxed and my heart slowed to normal. I found the keys to the cabinet.

Before I placed the knife in the drawer, I checked to make sure the hairbrush still resided behind the files. It was still there.

I heard the main door rattle. Probably Maggie. She was usually the first one here, if I wasn't. I needed some coffee, and good ole Maggie would set me up. I hurriedly shoved the knife in with the hairbrush, slammed the drawer and locked it.

—hey knife, you come to hide as evidence to? Boy that good old Grant sure doesn't want to be caught. Oooh, nice blood—

The front door creaked open, then shut. High heels clicked across the floor. They stopped for a second. Then they started again and they got louder and louder. Maggie approached my office.

There was a knock at the door just as I got to my chair. "Come in," I said.

Maggie entered. "Morning Grant."

"Hey."

"You okay?"

"Yeah, why?"

She squinted. "You're sweating."

"Am I?" I wiped my brow. "Wow, I am." Now that she brought it to my attention, my armpits were damp and I could feel rivulets of sweat collecting on my chest hair.

"I'm okay," I said, but she didn't believe me.

"You need anything?"

"How about some coffee?"

"You sure?" she asked. "You sure you need the heat?"

"I'm fine, Maggie."

"Okay." She slowly turned and waited a second to see if I needed anything else, then left.

She shifted some things around on the food cart and a minute later, I heard the coffee brewing. Good, her mind was on work.

With the paper out, things usually settled down the following day and today would be no exception. I needed some time to figure some shit out.

"Maggie," I called.

She returned.

"Make sure that I'm not bothered for the rest of the morning. I don't care what issues there are, they can wait until the afternoon."

"Um, okay." She sounded awfully confused and I felt a twinge of guilt leaving her out of the loop. "If you need me for anything, let me know."

"I will. Thanks."

She left again and shut the door behind her.

I trusted that she would let me have the time I requested. She could be a hardass sometimes. The others would probably bug me despite my demand—especially Pete—but with Maggie as my backup, I was assured.

I turned on my computer. It beeped. I waited for a moment until it fully booted, then loaded up Internet Explorer. My Yahoo homepage popped on. The cursor blinked in the search box.

What exactly should I type? I wasn't sure.

But within seconds, I was sure.

CHAPTER SIX

1

I typed in **SCREAMING GHOSTS** and tapped enter. Yahoo's fast search engine displayed over 1 millions searches on the screen. The first one had a heading entitled 'Screaming Ghosts, or Banshees'. The site was Wikipedia, which I have used before as a source in my editorials and articles. Using Wikipedia as a major source wasn't very professional, but it's quick and usually contained the facts I needed. Besides, none of my non-Internet using readers who do care were probably reading the *Tribune* anyway.

'Screaming Ghosts, or Banshees as they are commonly called, have origination in Irish folklore. Most of the time these ghosts are women and signify some sort of impending doom, generally death. Chances are if you see one or a Banshee stares you down, your survival is not good. The loud and high pitch Scream is proportionate to the degree of that doom. A general rule of thumb is if you have

to cover your ears, then you will probably
die. Anything less most likely just means
something painful but bearable. You might think
that you can send these ghosts back by trad-
itional methods like helping them complete tasks
or finding someone they love to tell them how
much they love them, etc. But Banshees are a
different sort. As of this writing, there is
nothing concrete someone can do if a Banshee
is terrorizing you.

Not all Banshees are bad. There are some
who go about their supernatural existence
with daily routines as if they were alive.
they will go to work, pursue their recreations,
and be peaceful like nothing ever happened. You
don't have to worry about these, just the ones
that scream.

Some Banshees leave objects behind that were
important to them when alive.
usually this object they treasured until the
day they died or it was an object of someone'sthey
didn't want to forget.

RELATED WEBSITES
www.ghosthunterjones.com
www.irishfolklore.com
www.bansheedeathcount.com'

That's what I see; it had to be. A Banshee was
running loose in Ilton and I seemed to be the only one that
knew about it. Well, me and those who saw her just before
they died. Miss Molly, Old Man Noonan, Betty. What did
they see before they passed away?

I looked over the related websites again and clicked on *www.bansheedeathcount.com* because it appeared the most interesting. The page downloaded and 70% of the website was ads. There were some options to add your own sightings and include any loved ones or friends you believed have died from a Banshee vision. In the middle of the web page was a large box with 'TOLL' scripted in red block letters. The number currently read '842 since 2005'. That didn't seem so bad. An insensitive thought, but more people probably have died from slipping in the bathtub since 2005.

For an interesting-sounding web site name, the actual site was dreadful. I backed up to the Wikipedia site and clicked on *www.ghosthunterjones.com*.

A solid black page appeared with just a phone number in white in the center of the page. *1-219-433-2691*. And that was it.

"Oooooh," I mocked. "Mysteeeerious…"

I jotted the number on a Post-it and stuck it to my monitor.

A door slammed. Through the window, I watched Bobby storm through the office. Maggie yelled at him to stop, I wasn't to be disturbed. He said something to the effect of fuck you and continued. He whipped open my door with Maggie in tow.

"I'm sorry," she said. "I tried to tell him."

"It's okay, Mag."

Bobby shut the door when Maggie left.

2

"I need to talk to you," Bobby said.

"I figured, you coming in here like some kind of bastard." I shut down my computer.

"Well, shit is pointing to you."

"What are you talking about?"

Bobby sat down. "I'm missing some evidence."

"Why does that point to me?"

"You're the only one who knows about any of the evidence."

"Am I? You're one hundred percent positive?"

We stalemated a gaze. I broke it first.

"Okay," I said, "I'll bite. What's missing?"

"The hairbrush."

I attempted to hide any knowledge of the hairbrush from my face and I wondered if Bobby saw that. Five, four, three, two, one...

"Really? Why do you think it has something to do with me?"

"As I said before," Bobby said, "You're the only one who knew about any of the evidence, especially the hairbrush."

"Especially the hairbrush," I commented. "So it's very possible that someone also could have known about the other evidence?"

"Maybe"

"Yes or no," I forced.

"Yes, it's possible."

"Then you can't be certain I'm the *only* one who knew about the hairbrush." I smirked and I knew he saw it. "Can you?"

He didn't answer and I saw a tiny look of defeat wash over his face. I decided he's had enough of my big-time fancy questioning.

"So. How the fuck would I get into your evidence locker?" I asked.

He laughed. "Seriously? Have you seen what I'm working with as far as a police station? My 'evidence locker' is an old metal filing cabinet with no lock."

I caught a quick glance to my own cabinet, then back to Bobby.

"Why would you take it? That's what I don't understand," he said.

After getting up, I walked to my office door and opened it. "Leave. I can't believe you are accusing me of taking a piece of shit hairbrush."

It seemed like an hour before Bobby stood up. *Finally.* Was he trying to break me? It was going to take more than a minute of remaining still.

"Something crazy is going on here in Ilton," he said, "And I know I'm some hick Chief of Police, but I know something crazy is happening. You might be involved and you might not. Either way, I will find answers."

"Then you find them. Find them right out of my office."

Bobby left my office and I watched him until he was completely gone. He gave Maggie a flirtatious glimpse. She nodded once. Good girl.

Maggie appeared in my office seconds later.

"What was that about?" she asked.

"Nothing. Just got a bug about something. Needed to vent."

She didn't believe me. She smelled my bullshit even before I said it. "That's no bug, Grant."

"I know," I muttered. "I know."

Maggie didn't leave.

"Not now, Maggie. Not now at all."

"Then when? Whatever you got going on inside here—" She tapped her brain. "—you obviously can't do it alone. You need to share it."

She was right, I know that, but I couldn't bring her into everything. Everything that may hurt her.

"No, Maggie. *Not now means not now—*"

"Fine." She whirled around and walked through the door.

"Maggie—!" I called out after her.

Useless of course. I really didn't want her to come back so I would have to yell at her again. But I did have to tell someone. At least to get some advice on what was going on in this town.

I peered at the phone number written on the yellow Post-It stuck to my monitor.

3

Someone picked up the phone on the second ring. A cell phone. I heard the cackle of bad reception.

"Hello?"

"Uh, hey. Is this…uh…ghosthunter?" I felt weird saying it, but I had no other name for this guy or any other information than what the website provided me.

A pause. "Yup."

Was this guy going to give me more? "I found your number from website."

"Okay. Whatchya got?"

"I'm not sure."

"Well, is it a ghost at least?" A little sarcasm?

"At least. I just don't know. I don't know what's going on. I really don't know what I've seen."

"You don't know much do you."

Bastard, I thought. "I know your fucking website popped up when I searched for banshees."

Another pause.

"Hello?" I said.

"Banshees?" I heard on the other end. His tone quickly got serious. "You said banshees, didn't you?"

"Yes."

"Um…" Some thinking perhaps? "Look, I'm in Florida right now. Where are you?"

"Ilton. Illinois. About sixty miles South of Chicago." I always had to add that little bit about sixty miles south of Chicago because you could say Ilton, but no one would have a clue where it was. Even the Illinoisans who lived in the vicinity didn't even know.

"I see. Not bad," he said. "Not bad. Is it serious there?"

"Three people have died."

"Very serious I'd say." I heard paper rustling in the background. "I can be there in three days. I've got to finish up some business here. What's your address?"

I gave him my address. "You don't think this is a prank call, do you?"

"You don't sound fake my friend. You sound like something serious is happening there and you're afraid." He nailed it.

"That's right."

"Good. Three days. What's your name?"

"Grant," I said.

"I'll see you then."

Like a silent jet whizzing by, Ghosthunter Jones was off the phone.

I didn't even get his name.

4

The next couple of days went by uneventful. I wrote my next couple of editorials just to get them out of the way. My guys (and Maggie) went about their journalistic duties gathering stories and tidbits of information for future stories like good little reporters. I didn't talk much to them, especially Maggie. I think after the day I told her I wanted to be alone, she shied away from bothering me on other things. She no longer asked about my day or my night or if I saw this episode of that TV show. She would come into my office and drop papers off without a single hello.

Did she see something in me? Did she know about everything? Did she know about how Bobby thought it was me? They seemed to have gotten a little chummy recently. Just how chummy was another mystery that would have to wait.

Maggie and I use to be chummy. That was four months ago. We had a year of fun and, I'll admit, love. If you asked her I'm sure she'd say she enjoyed the fling. A fling. What a way to put it.

Now we were Boss and Worker. I told her what to do and she did it. And despite that *I* was giving the order, she still happily carried out any task I gave her.

We didn't end on a terribly happy note. One night I had cooked an Italian dinner—you know the great bachelor dinner of spaghetti, salad, garlic bread, and green beans— and she said after a forkful of wrapped pasta, "I don't think I could fall in love with you. It's already been a year and I'm not in love." She's the kind of person who liked to stick her fork in and spin it in the spaghetti to start a ball going. Then she lifted it out and continued to spin the fork until the spaghetti was wrapped around the fork enough where she could place it in her mouth. Anal with a hint of conformity.

"Did you now just realize this?" I had said.

"No, months ago, but I figured I'd give this a longer chance."

I dropped my utensils. "Well, thanks...I guess..."

I mean, we didn't argue or yell at each other. I just removed myself from the table and disappeared into my bedroom.

Even at work the next Monday, we remained amicable. Two days didn't fester into anything. Maybe I wasn't in love with her as much as I thought. That's possible since I let her go so easy.

But with Bobby traipsing in here like he owned Maggie and getting all chummy

—mystery chummy mystery chummy—

Twinges of jealousy rocked my body each time I saw them together.

Did I still have something for her? Well, yeah, of course I did. She's a great woman. Very affectionate, loving, and loyal. Awesome in bed. Not great, or good, or adequate; Maggie was exceptional in bed. I missed that, but I also missed the other qualities I fell in love with. I guess I was still deeply in love with her.

Shit, I needed to get out here. Sometimes seeing her and working with her made me nostalgic for the times we had. I needed some of *Betty's Grub*.

5

The afternoon quickly turned cloudy. Storm clouds gathered in the distance. Dark gray, loopy clouds just begging for the rain to be released. Good, deep storm clouds…the kind that spawned tornados if the dew point was higher.

The walk to *Betty's Grub* usually took me about five minutes, but I strolled today. Today was a strolling day. No hurry to get some food; just a little hurry to get away from the paper, from Maggie. How did one loser Police chief named Bobby Hamilton make me so jealous?

I turned the corner onto Main Street. The restaurant looked packed. My watch read 2:29. Afternoon brunch crowd? I doubted the farmers and clientele in the area ate brunch.

The gold-plated cowbell dinged when I walked through. The crowd inside all glanced up at me. A decent crowd, not as many as the cars outside indicated, but still a decent crowd.

One old guy raised a finger to me in hello. I didn't recognize him and still couldn't place him as I took a booth near the front corner. The closest people were a few tables away, which is how I kinda wanted it.

Kara came over. "Hey," she said.

"Hi. How are you?"

"Okay, I guess."

"Yeah. It sucks."

"Mm-hmm. What can I get you?" She poised her pencil over her pad.

"What's wrong?" I asked.

"Nothing. You gonna order? It's kinda busy and I got other tables."

"Kara, something's wrong."

She nervously looked back at everyone else. "I shouldn't even say this." Kara plopped down opposite me.

"Say what?"

A couple of the locals eyed Kara suspiciously, then eyed me suspiciously.

"People are talking about you."

"I'm use to that," I said. I was. People either hated you as an editor or loved you. I'd like to think the majority of the town loved me, but there were always a few that expressed their disdain for me.

"No. About Betty, and the others," Kara whispered.

"What about them?"

She looked back at the others. "They are saying you had something to do with their deaths."

"Had something to do with them—"

"Not exactly," Kara said quickly. "But that you actually killed them."

"What?"

"I hear a lot. You know I do."

"I know. But you also know that it's ridiculous right?"

She didn't answer.

"Kara?"

She nodded. "I know. I wouldn't be talking to you if I thought it was crazy."

"Thank you. Now just get me my usual and make sure you get back to the others. They might think we are having an affair."

Kara smiled and got up, shier than usual, and went to check on her other customers.

Kara believed the rumors a little bit. Not a lot, just enough to be scared to talk to me. Just enough to avert her eyes from me. Just enough to make me feel like the outcast of Ilton.

A few of the farmers gave me some of those familiar disdained looks, but I didn't care right now.

Kara brought my food a moment later, but I didn't really enjoy it with the others watching me, glaring at me. I finished quickly, tossed Kara a good tip, then left.

CHAPTER SEVEN

1

What else could I do but leave *Betty's Grub*. The stares were too much to handle and I've handled a lot in my life. My mother's death, my father's death, my brother's...dammit, I promised myself years ago I would forget about that. My brother. He died a long time ago. No sense in trying to remember that.

My office door was open and currently blocked off by a weathered brick. The humidity hung in the air, but a little breeze swirled. Sometimes the air conditioner didn't kick on at the right moments, so I guessed this moment called for a propped door.

Pete greeted me first when I arrived. Did I really want to be here? No, but I couldn't really ignore my staff or that thing called a job.

"Hey, Pete, how's it going?" I asked just out of courtesy really, not because I cared.

"Okay." Instead of going back to what he was doing, he kept a watchful eye on me.

Maggie stopped me before I got to my door.

"Grant, there's someone in there to see you."

"Who?"

"Don't know," she said, shrugging.

"Well did he introduce himself? What am I getting into?"

"I don't know. No need to get snippy."

"Snippy? Does anybody use that fucking word anymore?"

She didn't respond. Maggie turned and huffed away.

I put my hand on the doorknob and felt the eyes of my staff drilling into my back. What nerve do they have? Hell, I didn't even know who was in my office. What made them think that I did?

Sitting in the chair in front of my desk was the man who didn't introduce himself to Maggie. He had white hair and a salt-speckled, dark beard peppered his face. His greasy hair was matted to his head, like he hadn't washed it in days. The man turned and when he saw me, he smiled.

"Hello, I'm Mavis Jones."

As soon as he said his name, it hit me. "The ghosthunter."

"Yup."

I shut the door. "I'm glad you could make it," I said. I stuck out my hand. "I'm Grant."

"Yes, I figured."

"Would you like some coffee or something?"

"Let's get down to the banshee."

I sat at my desk.

"I want to see the site of the first vision," Mavis said.

"Now?"

"Why not? I want to know that atmosphere as soon as possible."

"I suppose. What do you think you'll find?"

He shrugged. "I can take some readings and such."

I smiled.

He returned the smile. "You're a little skeptical, aren't you?"

"A little."

"I'll make you a deal. After you take me to the site and I take my little readings, I will show you some things that might make you think differently."

I waited for a punchline, but he didn't speak again. He was serious.

"Okay," was all I could say.

2

I drove Mavis quickly through town so anyone walking wouldn't get their curiosity, and more importantly, their suspicions up. It was bad enough they suspected me of killing a few beloved townspeople, but I didn't need them wondering about a random stranger I was toting around. I could hear the whispers now: "Hey, that killer is driving around an accomplice," or "The editor is probably going to 'edit' that stranger if you know what I mean," or maybe even "Who do you think he'll kill next?" It's asinine how—

"Grant?"

I broke from my ridiculous trance and saw the car veering too much to the right and heading for the shallow ditch. I jerked the wheels back and got the car completely on the road again.

"You okay?" Mavis asked.

"Yeah, just thinking."

He paused when I didn't continue. "And just what were you thinking about?"

I shrugged. "My life in Ilton. Ilton. My future in Ilton."

"Small town blues?"

And in those three words, I heard that he knew exactly what and how I was thinking. My thoughts were 'blue' for sure, but he seemed to sense something more. Something he had either seen or experienced before. I wasn't sure if now was the right time to ask, or pry.

I looked over and watched him peer out the window. No, this wasn't the right time, even though my curiosity was peaked. And no, not because I was a reporter, but because I was a compassionate human being.

I'd ask him later. We could get drunk and I could ask him and he would spill all. Just like a drunken girl spilling her clothes. That sounded like a plan.

"Is this it?" I heard him ask.

I focused my eyes. I had unknowingly slowed down. This was it. How the hell did I do this without thinking?

"Yeah this is it."

I pulled into the short, grassy field entrance and shut off the car. Mavis hopped out and opened the rear door. He pulled out his bag of supernatural investigating goodies.

Me? I still sat in the car.

"You coming?" He asked.

"Give me a sec," I said.

"Okay. I'll wait."

He made his way to the front of the car, set the bag on the hood and propped his butt on the grill.

Life seemed to be guttural, and by that I mean life could sometimes be a low grunt that came from deep within, to escape through your mouth and then into the air, into nowhere. Right now, that's what I thought life was like. My life. I lived in my hometown; I was the editor of this hometown's paper which had maybe 100 readers. I was including readers that buy the paper at the grocery store and the one gas station *and* those who had a subscription. I ate daily at *Betty's Grubs* while trying to maintain my sanity in this town. Bobby was right. Forsaken was the perfect word for this town when you've lived in it all your life or, in my case, all but three years.

That aside, I was now accompanying a man that I called to investigate a banshee. A banshee in Ilton? Sounded like bullshit. But then again, here I was only feet away from the man who was only listed as *GhostHunter Jones* on his website.

Through the window, I saw him glance at me. He probably wondered if I was going crazy in here. Well, yes, I was, but Mavis "The Ghosthunter" Jones didn't need to know that. Hell, I didn't even want to know that.

I removed the keys from the ignition and got out of the car.

"Everything okay?" He asked.

"You sure ask that a lot," I answered.

He laughed. "You seem to need to *be* asked that."

"I'm fine." I shut the door, then peered out into the gathering of trees. "Let's go check this out."

I started heading towards the trees and I felt Mavis pause before I heard him pick up his pack and slide off the car. I didn't want to look back and see him staring at me, a fellow who wasn't sure he wanted to find out any more about the floating woman who has haunted me the past few days.

When I heard his feet crunching against the dry leaves and branches, I figured he just wanted to concentrate on the banshee.

3

For the third time in a short amount of time, I stood at my campsite again. Everything was still in its original state since Chief Bobby Hamilton first came out to accuse me of some kind of mayhem. My tent was still set, my camping chair sat innocently by a long defunct fire area and the air was admittedly chillier than just a second ago.

Mavis noticed it too. He stopped and looked towards the sky. No clouds, no breeze. No way it was possible.

"Feel that?"

I nodded.

He removed a tape recorder

—No Grant No—

and clicked it on.

"About a ten to fifteen degree drop in temperature," he said into the recorder, "in a twenty foot radius."

He set down his bag and took out a couple of instruments. Ghosthunting instruments I assumed.

The first was a long needle attached to a shoebox-sized black box with a couple of wires. The needle looked like one of those knitting needles my mom used to use. It was silver and about the length of my forearm. Mavis flipped a switch and it powered to life, a few red lights blinking on. A gauge, like an audio gauge, lit up and the needle contained within jumped to life.

The next little ghosthunting tool was already clicking as Mavis pulled it out of the bag. *Click-click-cli-cli-cli—*

"Is that a Geiger Counter?" I asked.

"Yeah, sort of. I want to measure the air."

"Ghosts give off radiation?"

"Depends on the species."

Species? I didn't know there were species of ghosts. Mavis talked like he was a fucking scientist collecting samples of animals or shit. Species of ghosts? Was it possible this guy was more wacked than me?

"What's that other thing for?"

He held up the needle. "This is for…well…it's hard to explain."

"For what I've seen? You can explain it any way you can."

Mavis searched for words, but nothing came.

"What are you doing to do with it?"

He stood. "Well, I'm going to put this needle into the trees, the ground, plants. Stuff like that."

"What?"

"Keep an open mind."

"Mavis, trust me on this: I have an open mind."

"I'm going to read the area through the fauna." He sighed. Probably more for the fact I thought he *was* as crazy as me; but however he got his shit done, that's his business.

"Interesting."

"Open mind, Grant, open mind."

He picked up his Geiger Counter again and waved it around. First up, then to his left, then towards the ground. It *clicked* heavilyy in certain areas, and lightly in others. Once he got a general reading of the area, he followed the heavier clicking towards my tent. He stopped, knelt down and scooped a handful of dirt into a small baggie. He poked the counter into my tent, but the counter remained silent.

Mavis headed towards the area where I saw the woman, but the counter barely added any extra clicks.

"That's where I saw her."

"Really?" Mavis swung his counter around, maybe hoping for some other reading, but nothing happened. Nothing at all.

He scraped some leaves and dirt into another baggie and wrote something on the plastic with a Sharpie. Probably, 'Area where weirdo Grant supposedly saw a banshee...oh yeah, Grant's a weirdo'.

Mavis set down the counter and picked up the other instrument. Now we were getting to the good stuff. This was the instrument I had to keep an open mind about. Let's see what this baby did.

After picking out a tree, Mavis walked over and jabbed the needle into the tree. It didn't go in very far. Mavis then produced a rubber mallet

—this guy was Swiss Army Ghosthunter Jones—

and pounded the needle until an inch of it stuck out. He set the box down and made sure the wires were safe, then turned a dial on the box. The machine whirred to life again. Soon, a thin line of ticker-tape started popping out of the end.

At first, Mavis was nearly motionless, checking the tape and then adjusting the needle. It took about a minute for him to muster any reaction, but when he did, I thought he had shit himself.

When there was about ten feet of tape on the ground, he snatched up a portion and ran his finger along the jagged EKG-like lines. He repeated the same motion over the same portion about five times.

"Fuck," he muttered.

I loved a Ghosthunter that can curse. "What's wrong?" I managed without smiling.

"Nothing's wrong. Just the readings…" He trailed off as he read more of the tape. "This is new to me."

"What do you mean 'new'?"

Mavis looked up. "I'll be honest. I have been using this thing for about five years now and this is the first time that I've actually gotten some sort of reading. I mean, I guess I can call it a reading. It's something."

"First time?"

He nodded. "First time. I am shocked, surprised, amazed, confused…I don't know what to make of this."

"Are you skeptical of the readings?"

He didn't answer. Instead, he plucked out the needle and slammed it into the next tree. Rubber mallet, pound, and more ticker tape.

After a minute with that tree, he took a reading from another tree. And another. And another. And another.

When he seemed finished with the trees, he jammed the needled into the ground near a crowded patch of plants. Weeds actually. Tall stalks of grass, dead brush, and those little pricklies you stepped on when you're mowing the grass.

Apparently the same kinds of readings were coming from them also.

"Listen, Mavis, you must realize how Goddamn curious I am now," I said.

"I know, I know."

Then, the tape stopped. No lines, no beeps, no clicks.

"That's it," he said.

"What's it?"

"They are telling me nothing more."

"They?"

"The fauna. The trees, the plants. They are done talking."

I chuckled. "Well, do we need an interrogation room, a bright light and a good cop, bad cop plan?"

Mavis smiled. At least I hadn't offended him.

"A few years ago, scientists believed that plants can 'talk'. That they could witness things, feel things and sense everything going on around them."

"So you are saying that when you talk to plants, they are listening?"

"Sort of." Mavis gathered up his equipment and placed them back in the bag. "I'm done here."

Back at the car, I looked back at the line of trees. *Did they see what I saw? If they feel, did they feel what I felt? Fear? Do plants feel fear?* I knew that I sure felt fear and sadness, but the plants?

"To prove their theory, the scientists decided to try and solve a murder purely by botanical means," Mavis said. He laid his bag in the back seat. "A mother and child had been brutally killed and it was two weeks with no leads and no clues. The scientists took any plants that were in the room where the murder occurred and brought them into their lab. The police brought all their suspects into a line-up one by one and as the suspects walked through and did their little turnabouts and shit, the scientists took readings of the plants.

"There was one suspect in particular that elicited similar, chaotic readings from all the plants. And based on that, the police interrogated the suspect harder and eventually he confessed to the murders.

"It sounds odd, but it worked. The scientists were labeled heroes and they have been asked to do investigations all over the world, but there was one problem. Despite the accurate readings and the lucky interrogation, no court in any country would accept plants as credible witnesses. The scientists were testing a theory and it only *happened* that one of the suspects brought into the line-up admitted to the murders. Circumstance and luck. That's all it was. Some believe the police had some evidence against the perpetrator, which was enough to bring them in, but not enough to charge him, and continued to barrage the guilty one until he cracked."

"Yes, but a theory was tested and proven, right?"

"Don't you wonder why you haven't heard of this story before I just told it?"

I nodded.

"Most of the scientific community laughed at the scientists and they haven't done anything with the testing since."

"So why do you use it?"

"I use it to see if plants will relay any recent changes to their environment. It's a very plausible study."

"How do you know? If this is the first time you received any readings, how do you know?" I interviewed him like a reporter. I was in newspaper mode.

"I don't know. I guess I just believe."

"You are a walking *X-Files* episode."

We both paused, but then broke up in laughter. We both got into my car.

"I guess that means you believe me, right?" I asked.

"I do, Grant. I sure do."

"Thank you."

He smiled. "You guys got a hole-in-the-wall diner in this shithole town?"

"You are asking the right man. We sure do."

4

The ride back to town was quiet. I didn't really expect a lot of conversation. Mavis took some readings and samples and I watched and eventually heard some crazy story about a plant who fingered a murderer. Did they have witness protection for plants?

"God, this town is your typical Midwestern town," Mavis said, breaking the silence. "What the hell do you do here?"

"I run the newspaper…that's all I do."

"I mean for fun."

"I run the newspaper…that's all I do."

Mavis snickered. "Yeah, fun times."

"We don't have the places you Big City folk do."

"Tell me you have a bar at least."

"One. The Tavern."

"Original." Mavis sat up in his seat. "Stop."

When I didn't stop, he grabbed my arm.

"Stop," he said forcefully.

I eased the car next to the sidewalk. "What?"

"One house back. Something in the window," he said.

I looked back. Miss Molly's house. "What did you see?"

"I don't know. Something in the upstairs window. We have to go inside."

I shook my head. "We can't. It's part of a police crime scene."

"Why?"

"One of the deaths happened in there. Miss Molly."

"Perfect." He was already starting to get out of the car.

"We can't get caught in there. County is on the case."

"Not your local boy?"

"Don't get either of us started—"

Mavis hopped out and grabbed his bag. More plant readings I suppose. I did a quick mental inventory of Miss Molly's bedroom.

"I don't think there were any plants in the room she died."

"Oh," he mumbled. He put his bag back in my car. "Well, I still want to check it out."

I don't think I was going to convince Mavis not to go in there. I checked the street and it was quiet and uninhabited by anyone at the moment. "Okay, let's—"

But Mavis was already in Miss Molly's yard.

5

We headed up the porch and peeked into the windows on each side of the front door. The house took an even darker view in broad daylight. I remembered what I had found in there the last time I was inside and didn't really want to go back.

"Look, you care if I wait out here? Just in case someone questions why two guys are—"

"I want you inside. I need a tour guide."

A tour guide? What the hell?

"The door is probably already unlocked," I said, defeated. Looks like I had no choice.

The door *was* unlocked, which goes to show you how careless County was.

The air in the foyer was different. I couldn't put my finger on it, but it was different somehow. Colder maybe, but that wasn't it. Thicker? Hard to exactly say what my senses told me changed from my last visit.

The hall to the kitchen seemed dimmer. Was someone here after me and before us? I thought that the hallway light was on when I came earlier. Maybe I turned it off and just forgot. I was always doing that when I was seven and I was still doing it now. My mom would have had a fit. Miss Molly would probably have had a fit.

"The bedroom?" Mavis asked.

I pointed to the stairs. Mavis slowly took the steps one at a time, each time checking the top of the stairs.

I followed and felt the air getting colder still.

"Temperature change," Mavis said. Probably to him, but I couldn't tell.

"I feel it." I needed to respond. To fill the air with something besides weirdness, silence and cold.

I was about five steps behind Mavis. He reached the top of the landing and motioned for me to stop.

"What?" I whispered.

"Nothing. Just being cautious."

Right. Cautious.

I joined him.

"Lead the way," he said.

Lead the way. I didn't want to. Ghosthunter Jones got a bug under his hat about something he saw in the window. Fucking bug.

Then we heard it.

6

It wasn't loud. More of a whisper, like someone's mouth inches from my ear telling me all the things I wanted to hear. Turning me on; erotic. A sound that I really wouldn't mind listening to all night—

"Grant!"

Mavis broke my trance. I could do without *that* kind of voice in the middle of the night.

"Sorry," I said.

"Then you heard it."

I nodded.

Mavis followed the sound, which came from the bedroom. I didn't have to lead the way now.

7

Mavis stepped through first and he moved forward enough for me to stand behind him.

"This is where that Miss Molly died?" He asked.

"Not *that* Miss Molly. Just Miss Molly."

"Miss Molly, got it."

"Yes. Right over there I believe," I said, pointing.

Mavis knelt down and shook his head. County had cleaned up the scene, so there probably wasn't enough of anything for Mavis to go on.

I looked around. Just as I remembered, no plants.

He stood. "I swear there was something in here."

"Do you really expect that whatever you saw was just going to casually wait for your arrival?"

"That would have been nice."

"You done?"

But before he could answer:

Another scream. And it *was* a scream this time. Not that whisper I yearned for when I heard the shrilling

—fingers scraping against chalkboard a car shrieking when the fan belt wasn't working brakes worn and scratching against the rotor incessant alarm at 7 a.m. ehh-ehh-ehh-ehh—

I wanted to squeeze my head off. Pop it like a zit so that sound would disappear. That sound was a blackhead on my brain.

"Fuck!" Mavis yelled. He was trying to plug his ears, but I knew that was useless. The sound knew how to get inside you no matter what you did.

My head swam from the pitch of the sound and even though I squinted just to keep from fainting, I still saw her floating towards the window from the outside.

"Mavis!" He looked at me. I pointed a finger to the window. He turned his head and I thought that, once again, he had shit himself.

The red-headed woman hovered right in front of the window, staring at me. First me, then Mavis. She acted confused. Like what the fuck were we doing here? This was her place now that Miss Molly was gone. This was her bedroom and her scream was the way she marked her territory. Her scream was her dog's piss. Dog's piss that you were being forced to drink.

Then she came through the window. As easy as that, as if we had opened the window for her to come on through. The scream subsided and Mavis and I were looking silly with our fingers in our ears and no sound.

"Shit, Mavis."

"That's her?"

"Yes."

Then he said something, but I didn't hear him. His mouth moved and dammit if I couldn't even read his lips. I didn't have that skill. If he screamed, I'd be able to read that: open mouth, tongue flapping, facing turning red.

I felt the air get extremely heavy, like a five ton car had been dropped on my head and chest.

"What?" But I'm sure he was in the same boat as me.

He realized it. He pointed at himself, then at the woman.

I shook my head. I don't think I liked where his head was at. Maybe the heavy air was quickly getting to him, making him delirious.

He ignored me and stepped to the woman anyway.

She floated just inside the window and didn't move as Mavis made his way toward her. She rose a little and came back down, eyeing Mavis suspiciously.

That's fine because at least there was no screaming. I bet that Mavis wished he hadn't listened to me about the plants. I bet he wished he had his fucking instruments now.

I bet he wished he hadn't come to Ilton.

The woman still didn't move and Mavis continued to get closer. What was he trying to do? Pick her up? Did he have a great first line to use on her?

Hey, come here often? You are a fucking screaming girl, let's get out of this place and get lost in each others' dimension.

Mavis stopped inches from the woman. He reached up. Was he trying to fucking touch her? Of all the crazy things that have happened in the past week, Ghosthunter Jones trying to touch the alleged banshee had to take the proverbial cake.

"No!" I said it before I realized he wasn't going to hear it.

But apparently she didn't appreciate Mavis trying to touch her. She backed up towards the window.

Then her face changed.

With me, her face had been normal, pretty in fact. Except for being a damn screaming bitch, she was kinda okay to look at. But now, all that changed within a few seconds.

Her hair flared out, like a million little snakes ready to strike at a moment's notice. The face elongated. I didn't know any other way to put it. It got longer, thinner. Her eyes widened and I swear I saw them dilate, like she was real.

It was her mouth I was most afraid of.

When she opened her mouth, I expected a scream, but instead her lips expanded and separated into an inconceivable gap. I thought for a moment that I could fit in there if I really tried. Not that I would, but I could. Her teeth changed from hard chunks of calcium

—if they were that anyway cavities probably—

into strings of saliva cascading from her mouth onto Mavis' head.

I dashed to Mavis and grabbed his arm. I pulled him away, but he didn't seem to want to go right away. After putting all my weight into tugging, he stopped resisting and backed up to the door with me.

I reached behind me

—when did the door fucking shut we are living in the *Poltergeist* movie and we are going to die she was going to slowly reach out for us and yank us into her world and kill us—

and grabbed the doorknob and whipped the door open. Both of us kept our eyes on the woman just in case she decided that it was our time to become ghosts.

It wasn't.

As soon as we backed through the door, the woman changed back into her original form and gave us one final scream. It was short, but loud enough to drop us to our knees in aural pain.

Then, nothing.

We looked up at the same time and only caught the tail end of dissipating mist.

Gone.

"What the hell was that?" Mavis finally asked.

"Her. That was her."

"I figured that. What was she doing?"

"Being angry, I think."

"Agreed."

"Next time don't try to touch her. I'm pretty sure that's what made her mad."

"Again, agreed. Stop my ass next time."

"I tried. You couldn't hear me." I stood, letting my legs get used to standing again. That last scream nearly did it for me.

"Well, at least I know now that it's a banshee." He glanced down the hallway. "Anything I should know about the rest of the house?"

I shook my head. "Just that room."

8

"Hello?"

That greeting came from downstairs. It was familiar.

"Hello? Anyone here?"

Bobby.

"We have to go," I told Mavis.

He gave me a quizzed look.

"The police are here."

"What?"

"Someone must have called on us. Saw us go in."

From below, "Grant, I know you are in here. I saw your car down the street."

"There goes our night," I said.

"Let's just get our whippings," Mavis said.

How much could Bobby do to us? We were actually doing him a favor.

I heard his feet plodding up the stairs.

"Yeah Bobby!" I yelled down. "It's Grant."

Silence, then I saw his shadow appearing at the top of the stairs.

"Grant? What the fuck are you doing—?" He came into view and immediately stopped, checking Mavis out. "Who the hell is this?"

"This is Mavis Jones."

"Mmm-hmm."

Oh, this was not the time to start with me Chief Police Bobby Hamilton.

9

"Okay," Bobby said. "That's all fine, but *who* is he."

I decided to just tell him. "He's a ghosthunter."

Bobby didn't know what to say. I could tell he was processing the last few minutes in his head. "A ghosthunter?" he finally asked.

"Yes. I called him."

"So we got ghosts? In Miss Molly's house? You think Miss Molly's ghost is staying behind? You think she will be able to tell you who killed her?" he said condescendingly. Bobby was being a bigger ass than normal. I just wanted to get out of there.

"It's a personal favor to me," I said. "Trying to figure out some things."

"Trying to figure out those screams?" Bobby then asked seriously.

"More or less."

Mavis stuck his hand out. "Mavis."

"Yeah, I know," Bobby said. He shook Mavis' hand. "Bobby Hamilton. Chief of Police."

"Nice to meet you."

"Mmm-hmm." Wow, it was nice to hear that I wasn't the only one Bobby like to say that to. "You guys can't be here."

"That is my fault, Chief," Mavis said. "I thought I saw something and needed to check it out. I just need a few more minutes. Check the rest of the house."

"Did you find out what you saw?" Bobby asked.

"No. Just got ambushed with some screams." Mavis pointed to the bedroom. "In there."

"That's where Miss Molly died," Bobby lightly mentioned.

"I told him already," I said.

"Okay." Bobby glanced at Mavis, then looked back at me. "Only a few more minutes. Five. I'm going to make another round in 10 minutes or so. You better be gone or I will have to arrest you for trespassing. The town would love to see that, eh Grant?"

"Fuck off, Bobby."

"Thought so." As he went down the stairs, he added, "Five minutes."

10

"The Chief is a dick," Mavis said when we heard the front door shut.

"Tell me about it."

"I guess spending the night here is out of the question."

"Yup. You heard him. We can't be here in 10 minutes."

Mavis moved down the hall. "Well, the air has settled."

"Is that good?"

"I imagine. There's probably nothing more that's going to happen in this place tonight anyway."

If that meant Mavis was looking to leave, that would be fine by me. I don't know what was actually scarier: the floating woman, or Bobby sneaking into the house like that. Depending on the day, I may have taken my chances with the crazed banshee.

"Yeah, I don't feel like being here any more than I need too." I was already heading down the stairs.

11

Mavis joined me a couple of minutes later and we walked in silence to my car. Mavis kept sneaking little glances back to the house.

"You still thinking she'll reappear?" I asked.

"A little part of me."

"That's the fourth time I've seen her. I'm beginning to think she likes my attention."

We got in my car and I asked, "You still hungry?"

"Nah. Tired."

"Yeah. Let's go back to my house. I need a drink. And I got some food we could snack on if we get hungry. I feel like relaxing for a little."

"Sounds good. You have some heavy stuff?"

"I'm a journalist. Of course I do," I responded.

We laughed.

That would be the last laugh we would share for a couple of days.

CHAPTER EIGHT

1

A nap *was* in order.

I didn't know if that was going to be possible as we pulled up to my house.

Maggie sat on my porch, watching each car go by. When she saw my car, she stood and crossed her arms. Mad? She didn't look mad. More concerned actually.

"Unexpected company?" Mavis commented.

"Surprised, that's all."

"Maybe it has to do with work."

I doubted it. She hadn't been to my house since the night we...

"Maybe," I said.

I pulled the car to a stop. Maggie started coming towards the car, but noticed Mavis was in the passenger seat, then stopped.

Mavis hopped out. "I'll just go inside. Looks like she has something to discuss."

"Okay. Just make yourself at home. Eat, drink, be merry and all that shit."

Mavis strolled past Maggie and entered the house.

"Maggie, what are you doing here?" I met her on the sidewalk.

"I wanted to talk to you."

"Paper not going to make it out next week?"

"Has nothing to do with the paper, Grant."

"Let's sit," I suggested.

We went back to the porch and sat on the steps.

"Grant, what's been going on the past few days?"

"Just living," I replied. "Just living and trying to get past the deaths."

"We all are with *you*."

"If everyone's with me, why do they treat me like I'm the untrustworthy outsider?"

"That's not what I meant. Everyone in this town is trying to get over the deaths. Don't make this solely about you. At least not with the others. With me you can."

"What do you mean?"

"You've been more distant with me at work than you have ever been. Sometimes when I see you, you seemed rushed. Other times, scared. You won't talk to me. Sometimes you act like you don't even want to be around people."

"By people do you mean you?"

"You know fucking well what I mean."

Maggie rarely swore. When she did it was something serious. No jokes, no sarcastic little comments, no trying to make her smile. A swearing Maggie is nothing to be reckoned with.

"Do I?" I turned to face her. "Do I know? I knew you once. But now? I don't know."

"You did know me once, but it was your choice to stop knowing me."

"Really now. My choice? You do forget, don't you Maggie."

"That has nothing to do with then. I need to know what is going on. Why do people think you killed Miss Molly, Noonan, and Betty—?"

"Don't forget about Noonan's grandmother."

"What?"

"The forest. Never mind."

"You're acting strange, Grant."

"I believe I'm acting just fine. Trying looking into a mirror, Maggie. Try looking at your own soul."

She *humphed*. "What the hell is that suppose to mean? My own soul?"

"Why are you so concerned about how I've been acting all of a sudden?"

"I thought we were friends."

"Well, you sure had a funny way of being my friend the past few years."

"Work has to be work, you know this."

I knew it, but that's all it ever was. "I'm sure your new little boyfriend put you up to this." I tried to stop myself from saying it before it was out, but I couldn't. I said it and there was going to be either wrath or there was going to be nothing.

"'*My little boyfriend*'!?" She stammered.

Wrath, then.

"You have no idea what you are talking about," she said. "No idea at all."

"I see everything, Maggie. I am very observant."

"What do you see then?" She challenged.

If this was what she wanted, then so be it. "I see the way you look at him when he comes into the office. I see the way he looks at you. I see something between you and I don't know if it's love, friendship, or just his cock." I paused. "Probably his cock."

"It sounds like you're calling me a whore!" She cracked her hand across my cheek. The slap stung a little, but I'm sure the way my hand flew to my face I looked ridiculously dramatic.

"Not at all," I managed to say. "Just come clean with it, Maggie. You've probably been holding it back so I wouldn't get mad or jealous."

"You're already mad and I haven't even said anything."

"So it's true then."

She paused herself. I knew what was coming next. I knew what she was going to say. It would be just like getting stabbed, I could already tell. We haven't really been anything in a very long time, but I know it would be just like she was cheating on me.

"You already know what I'm going to say," she said.

Was she fucking reading my mind or what?

"I just want to hear it," I said.

"No you don't."

I did actually. I needed her to say it. To confirm my suspicions all this time.

"I do."

She turned the thought in her head. Maggie looked at me, searching for something that told her that I really didn't. When she didn't see anything,

"Bobby and I slept together," she said.

I didn't say anything.

"We are together," she added.

"How long?"

"I'm not doing details, Grant. I said what you figured was true. That's all I'm talking about."

"Fine."

Maggie stood. "That's not why I came over here; to tell you about me and Bobby."

—me and bobby mcgee—

I shrugged.

"I still care," Maggie said. "I still care about you Grant. I still care about what happens to you, about what I see happening to you."

When I didn't say anything, she took a few more steps away.

"I can still be here if you want to talk."

"Okay."

"Grant, I mean it."

"I heard you!"

She was hurt. Maggie turned around and walked away, not looking back once.

2

I entered my own house. I heard Mavis in my kitchen. He was running water and removing plates from my cupboard. The porcelain clinks grated my nerves. My footsteps on my hardwood floor grated my nerves. The blaring TV grated my nerves.

Drying his hands, Mavis emerged from the kitchen.

"Hey. Everything okay?"

"Yeah. Fine."

"You sure? You don't look fine in the face."

"I'm sure. Just tired."

"If you say."

—I say I fucking say just let it be let me be let me be in my room all alone maggie and bobby fucking her tits bouncing on his chest unless she likes it on the bottom or doggie style then her beautiful tits rubbing on the bed—

"Gonna go lay down in my bed, Mavis. Really tired."

"I'm making dinner."

How long had I known this guy? Less than a Goddamn day? He's already making me dinner in my own house? Best friends forever, that's me and Mavis

—me and mavis mcgee—
I needed to lie down badly.

3

Upstairs, I took off my sweat-stained shirt and
threw it into the corner on top of other unwashed shirts. I
shut the door quietly and stretched across my bed, looking
up at the ceiling, half-expecting the banshee to be up there,
ready to mount me and have ghost-sex with me.

But she wasn't there. Just the boring white ceiling
with nothing to offer.

Maggie just didn't understand that I was in love
with her. Since that night; since before that night.

What went wrong? It wasn't that night. Sure we
fucked, but there was a lot more emotion in that night than
I have ever had. It wasn't just about the sex. It was more.
It was in the heart. At the risk of sounding female, I made
love to Maggie with my heart that night. God that sounded
female. Tomorrow I'll probably have PMS and a menstrual
cycle.

So it was after that night. Something gradually built
a barrier between us. There was never another night. Hell,
there was never another day. Just work.

Work has to be work. Since then, *Work has to be
work.* That's all we've been. Fucking co-workers.

Between then and now, something.

Something that I definitely couldn't ask Maggie
about. I'd probably get another slap on the face.

This was ridiculous. I couldn't sleep. Thinking
about Maggie and sex and Bobby and her and sex. There
was no point in trying to relax up here with my thoughts.

Whatever Mavis was cooking smelled absolutely wonderful. I couldn't remember the last time something like this smelled this good in my kitchen. Oh, I could remember many days and nights where I would come home from a baseball game or practice and these kinds of smells would drift into my nose and send me into a drunken food fit. My mother would be in an apron having her way with the oven and the cutlery and the vegetables

—knock knock who's there Oedipus rex Oedipus rex who Oedipus rex my mom—

Much to my dislike, she used vegetables.

This was the same kind of smell that was now in my kitchen.

"Whatch you got cooking in here?" I asked after enjoying the smells.

Mavis jerked around. "Oh! Grant. Shepherd's Pie. Just found some stuff in your fridge and went from there."

That meant vegetables. Mavis and my mom and their vegetables.

"Smells good. I'm starved."

"Thought so," he said. "Be ready in about 20 minutes."

I opened the fridge and pulled out a beer. "Beer?"

Mavis nodded. "That's a start."

I flipped off the lid of a bottle of Miller Lite and handed it to him.

"Thanks."

I sat at the table.

"So Mavis, tell me something."

"Sure." He put his creation in the oven, turned the dial, and set the timer. "What would you like to know?"

"You."

"Me? What could I possibly have for you to know?"

"Oh come on. Tell me a ghost story. Surely ghosthunters have the best ghost stories."

"We do, we do, but nothing really interesting."

"Well just tell me about your first encounter. That should prove interesting."

5

"I was twenty-five and an apprentice to Yohainne McCormick. I know that sounds like a weird combination of names but he was Ukrainian and Scottish. So he was drunk most of the time, but he knew his ghosts and knew where to find them. He was getting on in his years and needed to take someone on to take over the business.

"And I say business because he was an old time Ghostbuster. Nothing like that movie makes them to be. Guys carrying nuclear devices to trap ghosts. Please. He used his wits and experience to find ghosts and get rid them.

"The year he turned sixty eventually became a detrimental year for him. There was a castle in Ireland that he was summoned to. The castle was owned by Baron Richlackey who also owned the land running one hundred miles in all directions. He owned the towns, the businesses, everything. This area was a modern day feudal system mixed in with a little modern day mob action.

"So that year Yohainne turned sixty he was summoned by the Baron. You don't turn the Baron down. This was during a time when loyalty ran rampant through the world and if you were caught with your hand in someone else's cookie jar when your boss's cookie jar gave you plenty, then bad things happened to you.

"Yohainne arrived not knowing why he was there. He brought me mainly for company at first, then as things started to happen, he was glad to have me along for protection and extra muscle because what we were about to encounter would take more than just us. I was lucky to just escape with a broken nose and a couple of shattered ribs. Yohainne was not so lucky. I'll just tell you that right now so you don't get your hopes up that everybody survived.

"Our first meeting with the Baron was our only meeting."

The Baron strode into the dining hall with clichéd abandon. He was tall with shoulder-length dark hair that curled outward. The Baron was young, around thirty, and it was odd to see someone around my age an actual Baron. We sat when he told us to.

The Baron spoke first. "I will get to the point. You are here to clean this castle of a ghost. The ghost is my father and it is time for him to go."

Yohainne sat forward. "Is your father dangerous? Why do you think he's here?"

"I don't care why he's here. I just want him gone. He's scaring everyone who works for me. He's a nuisance." The Baron waved over his butler. "Here is a quick dossier on my father. Hopefully it may help you figure out what you need to do to eradicate him."

Yohainne glanced over at me. I knew he thought something was wrong here, that we'd find more than necessary.

And we did. We found out why the Baron needed to rid the castle of the ghost. We found secrets that would soften the most hardened man alive. The details weren't important; just that the Baron was a most foul human being. Ghengis Khan was a saint next to the Baron, but we didn't have time to debate this comparison.

Let's just say the Baron didn't need his father meddling around the castle giving away all the family and business secrets for the world to know.

The Baron bid us a goodday. We were shown to our lavish rooms and left to our own accord. We were told the castle was open to us except for one room in the basement of the castle. Only the Baron was allowed in there.

Of course that meant that we would go down there to see what the deal was. Maybe that one room in the basement was the one room that would give us what we needed to get rid of the father.

Why didn't we say no? Or why didn't we just leave right away? The answer, to us at least, was very simple: money. The Baron offered us two million dollars. Half on arrival and half upon successful completion of our task. It simply came down to money. That was a pretty penny to Yohainne, so I quite understood why he didn't want to leave.

As soon as we figured the castle was quiet with inactivity, we set about our preliminary tasks: reconnaissance and note-taking. I followed Yohainne with a notepad and pencil and jotted down everything he said. I tried to at least. Sometimes he would get on this roll and I'd only get about half of what he said. I never told him that, I just wrote down what I could. I'm sure he knew but he never said.

"We are heading straight to the basement," Yohainne said.

It took us about twenty minutes to find the room. The door was padlocked in four places. At the bottom of the door, I saw a thin piece of wire.

"Master McCormick, look." I pointed it out.

Yohainne knelt down and followed the wire to the nearest corner by the door. It was attached to a plain black box.

"Some kind of detection device," he said. "This room is meant to keep everyone but the Baron out. Interesting."

He examined the padlocks. "Archaic locks, Mavis. Easily removed."

Yohainne dug into his suit jacket pocket and removed a thin piece of metal no bigger than a nail file. He tested its strength and, satisfied, began the process of picking the locks.

Where my master learned this trade was beyond me, but he had all four of the padlocks undone within two minutes. Next, he removed a small screwdriver and undid two screws from the black box. He lifted the cover and inside was another roadway of wires.

"Have you seen something like this before?" I asked him.

"Once before. I didn't successfully shut off the camera, but I learned I just didn't cut the right wire. Yellow is for video. Luckily, this type of device doesn't have audio."

Yohainne snipped a yellow wire and a tiny light dimmed and then finally went out.

"You ready, Mavis?"

I nodded.

The door opened inward. Yohainne made sure to step over the wire and then he reminded me to do the same. There was no light but it appeared to be a hallway of some sort.

Soon, Yohainne flicked on a flashlight and we *were* looking down a long hallway.

"I guess it's this way," he said.

"Are you sure you want to do this, Master Yohainne?"

He laughed. "Of course I do. When someone tells you *not* to go somewhere, then that is the first place you go. The Baron does not want us to find something and that something is obviously down here. That something could also be why his father is haunting this castle. Do you understand?"

He always said 'Do you understand' when he didn't think I was listening.

"Yes, I understand."

"Good, now let's continue. You hold the light." He handed me the flashlight and I aimed it down the hallway.

Except for a small bend to the right, the hallway was relatively straight. We went down a small incline after about three hundred feet. Another fifty feet and the hallway opened up into a medium-sized cavern.

I shone the light upward. The ceiling was about twenty feet up and made entirely of dirt. I shone the light ahead. Another hallway angled to the right and I saw no ending.

"This place underground?" I asked.

Yohainne didn't answer. I followed him with the light and saw that he was headed for the wall. "Mavis, bring the light over here."

I took a few steps and aimed the light in Yohainne's general direction. But I didn't take any more steps. What I saw was enough to stop a train.

I dropped the light and Yohainne was quick to race over and pick it up.

"You okay, Mavis?"

He didn't give me a chance to answer. He was back over to the wall.

The easiest way I can put what I saw was that there were tombs in this room. Lined up from wall to wall and from floor to ceiling. Tombs with bodies. Not skeletons, but bodies. Everyone laid to rest as if they had just popped off for a quick nap.

When I had regained my stomach, I was able to actually see how many bodies were in here. I counted 150 tombs in this room. The hallway ahead probably led to another cavern with more tombs and more bodies.

"Master Yohainne, this doesn't feel right."

"Of course not."

Something scrapped against the second hallway's walls. We both looked into the hallway. Yohainne removed a pistol from his jacket.

"Mavis, get behind me."

The scrapping quickly got louder.

"You think it's him?" I ask Yohainne. "The father?"

"Either him or the Baron and if it's the Baron, we are screwed."

There was a small grunt as a swirling mist started to enter the room.

"I don't think it's the Baron," he said.

Soon, a large human form followed the mist. It wasn't human, but that's the only way to give you a comparison of what it looked like. It floated above the ground and it had no legs. Just a torso and a head.

"There we go," I heard Yohainne say as if we was talking about the weather. He pulled a black and white photograph from his pocket and showed it to me.

"The father," he said.

The ghost turned around and entered the hallway again. It stopped and hovered there, its back to us.

"I think it wants us to follow him," Master Yohainne said.

Despite having the worse feeling of dread, I knew Yohainne was going to follow the father into the hallway. Into whatever sat at the end of the hall.

We followed and the hallway was nearly exactly the same as the first and even went on the same incline right before another cavern. This cavern was larger and appeared to hold more tombs. The father went to the center and hovered a little higher, giving us more light to see by. More tombs, more bodies.

"Master Yohainne, what is going on here?"

"I don't know. I don't know."

Behind me, I heard something else messing with the padlocks. "Shit, it's the Baron."

"Watch your language Mavis." He pointed to a tomb. "Quick. Get inside one of those."

"What?"

"Get inside one of the tombs and hide."

I walked to the nearest one and looked at the woman with long blonde hair who was about my height. She was very pretty. How did she keep like this? I climbed inside and had just enough room to shuffle myself over her body. I laid on the other side. I was able to look between her chin and the top portion of her neck and see Yohainne searching for a tomb he could fit inside. He scrambled between a few tombs, but the moment he stopped finding a hiding place, I knew something terrible was about to happen.

"Master!" I whispered.

He turned and raised his index finger to his lips. *Keep silent*, he mouth.

At that moment, the Baron walked in. Master Yohainne must have heard his footsteps. Those two words he spit through the air probably saved my life in that tomb.

"Yohainne," he said. "What are you doing in here?"

"Checking things out. My job."

"You were told not to come in here. This is very bad for you."

"It's obvious why you didn't want me to come in here."

"Yes, obvious," the Baron mumbled.

Then the Baron suddenly reached out and grabbed Yohainne's neck with both his hands. Yohainne didn't really know what hit him. The Baron pulled him closer and then smiled. He smiled big and then took a huge chunk from Yohainne's neck. The bite left a gaping hole.

Blood gushed in vast amounts. More than should be gushing.

I couldn't watch anymore. I turned my head away, hoping the Baron would just leave.

But I heard more skin ripping. I heard bone crunching. Blood spurted, splashing against the floor; the Baron's mouth squished whatever part of Master Yohainne remained inside. I heard everything that I didn't want to hear. Things that I hoped I would never hear again.

When all those sounds stopped, I turned by head back and watched Baron spit out a chunk of Yohainne.

The Baron tossed the remains of my mentor to the tomb's floor. I bit my lips, hoping the screams and the horror would stay inside of me. The Baron's eyes scanned the room; I knew he knew I was here somewhere, but he gave up in a matter of seconds.

The monster headed for the first cavern. I heard the outer door slide open and then shut. I listened for the padlocks, but nothing happened.

I stayed in the tomb for at least thirty minute before I decided to get out of the tomb. I tip-toed past Yohainne, trying not look, but I couldn't help it.

I couldn't tell it was Yohainne. I couldn't tell what was what on my former teacher. The gun was easy to spot. I picked it up just in case.

6

"Suffice it to say, I got out of there and ran to the closest town," Mavis said.

"Did the Baron catch you at all?"

"Well, almost. When I got to the town, there were some people that followed me, but I was able to catch a bus out of there and locate a town not owned by the Baron."

"Sorry about Yohainne," I said. "That's some story."

"My first experience. Hardly ghostly, but set me up for life."

"Have you ever been back to that castle?"

"Hell no. The Baron was a scary fellow. No way did I wanted to meet him again."

"I don't blame you."

"So you've been doing this a long time?"

Mavis nodded. "Thirty years."

"So what was the father? Just a simple ghost?"

"I think it was a banshee, but I never had the opportunity to investigate further." Mavis finished his beer. "Mind if I have another?"

"Go ahead."

"But banshees are rare. They are like the Holy Grail for ghosthunters."

"Which is why you rushed to this wonderful Ilton Township?"

"Yep. I'd be lying if I said it was for the interest of paranormal science."

"It's okay. I'm glad you're here."

"Thanks."

I stood up. "Look, I'm going to shower and change before I eat."

"Okay. I'll get it ready."

7

Honors History camping trip.

For doing a great job in the class, Mr. Hodgkins decided to take everyone camping. There were about 15 of us, including my girlfriend, Laura. She promised that something special would happen.

And to a 17-year-old, I hoped something special meant something sexual.

We went to the state park located about twenty miles from Ilton. It was hard to select who would be staying in whose tent since I wanted Laura to stay in mine, but it was boys with boys and girls with girls.

Everyone knew that during the night, things would switch. Boys with girls, and girls with boys. Laura with me.

But it was earlier than night. Most of the students had decided to go fishing except for me and Laura. We decided to hang back and stay in my tent for a few moments.

Which I hoped would start that something special.

Laura zips the tent shut and tells me to lie back. I did. She crawls to me and straddles me. I immediately get an erection.

Next, Laura slips off her t-shirt, exposing her black bra. Her breasts are shoved together and it looks like her nipples are ready to say hello.

"What's going on?" She playfully asks.

"Me is going on," I reply. "I'm going on and going up."

She laughs. "I can tell."

She pushes her pelvis into my erection and it feels nice.

Laura bends over and gives me a soft kiss, her tongue teasing my bottom lip.

"How would you like that tongue on your hardness?"

"Why the fuck would I say no?"

She eases back and slides back far enough to undo my pants. As her fingers latch on to the zipper, we hear An amazing shrill pierce the tent.

We both look outward, even though neither of us could see anything.

She removes her hands and grabs her shirt. "What was that?"

"I don't know," I say. "It sounded like it was right outside."

I lean up and wait until my erection goes down. I redo my pants and unzip the flap.

"Where are you going?" Laura asks.

Another shriek shoots through the tent.

"To see what that is."

"No, just wait. It'll pass."

"That's already twice, Laura. Someone might be in trouble."

I exit the tent and stand, looking around. Nothing looks out of the ordinary. I feel Laura emerge from the tent.

"Which way do you think it was?" I ask.

"I don't know. Don't care. I'm going to find the others."

"Fine."

I take off in the direction I think the scream is, but I'm not sure. It didn't sound natural. It actually sounded like—

I trip.

I trip on a fallen tree. Something moist starts soaking through my jeans on my knee. I look down: it's blood.

"Dammit!" I yell.

I wipe off the dirt and leaves that have attached to the blood-stained area and squeeze my knee. It doesn't hurt, so I figure everything is okay.

When I stand up, I see her.

And it is the same her that I saw hovering around my mother when she died and the same her that scared my father the time he died. Now she floats in front of me, glaring at me like I had done something horribly wrong.

Am I next?

Her gaze leaves mine and I watch her eyes aim for something behind me. I turn. Standing in the tall brush is Laura. She stands like stone, like me when I first saw the woman.

"Laura!" I scream. "Run!"

She doesn't move.

The woman's mouth opens and I knew what would happen, but I don't have time to plug my ears.

The shrill again.

That fucking shrill.

This time I am next to it and had no tent to absorb some of the noise.

But it is short this time.

—short sweet and to the point—

And I think the point is Laura.

"Laura! Run!"

Something snaps inside Laura. She looks at me, then the woman, then realizes what I had said because she does run. Within a few seconds she is out of eyesight.

I whip my head back around.

The woman is gone too.

8

I find Laura crying in my tent. Her eyes burn red from constantly rubbing the tears from her eyes.

As I enter the tent, she rubs again, harder. Some of the skin returns to its peach color, but the rest of it around her eye stays patchy red.

"Grant," she blubbers, "what was that?"

"I don't know." But I do know. I sure as fuck do know. What I don't know is what is going to happen next. I could make an educated guess.

"Laura, I want to you stay with me tonight," I ask.

"Why?"

"I need you to stay with me."

"You can't be thinking about that."

"Not that." I sigh. "Just to be safe from that thing."

She looks at me, probably trying to wonder if I was being serious about my request or if I really just wanted sex.

"Please," I beg.

"Okay."

I sit down. "Sit up," I command.

She does and I ease my way behind her. I straddle her so she can lean back between my legs into my chest.

"It will be okay, Laura. I promise."

"Okay."

It looks like that's all I am going to get out of her.

"We will just stay here all night until everyone is ready to leave in the morning," I say.

This time she just nods.

I don't realize how late it is because soon day turned into night...

And I must have drifted off to sleep...

9

I drift back into the real world by some kind of human scream. At first, I think it is HER, *but soon realize that it is one of my classmates. My eyes slowly open.*

Shit shit shit.

My arm flops to the side. I don't feel Laura.

Shit shit shit.

I perk up and check the tent: still no Laura.

"Laura!"

No answer.

"Laura!"

"Grant?"

It isn't Laura. Where the fuck is Laura?

Another scream, and then some chatter. My honors class.

I bolt from the tent but I am stopped by the scene before me.

All twelve of my classmates stand in a circle, their heads all down. I catch a glimpse of Mr. Hodgkins kneeling on the ground, checking something.

Greta is mumbling. "I saw...why didn't...I can't believe..."

I run over and break through the diameter.

"What's going on," I say. Then I look down and see Laura.

She is a bloody mess. Her body had been bent at the waist and she is arched backwards like in some weird and grotesque Yoga position. Her limbs tangle around each other. I don't know what her arm is and what her leg is. A huge gash runs from hip to hip on her belly and I couldn't tell now how, whoever did this, got her to bend like that.

"Oh my God," is all I could manage.

Greta hugs me, sobbing. "Grant. I saw her last night. She came from...your tent. I passed her right over there—" I feel her point, but I didn't look. "—she said she had to pee."

Mr. Hodgkins. "All right, class. I called emergency and they should be here any minute. Let's all go back to our tents and try to calm down."

A few turn and scatter back to their tents. Greta pushes back.

"Would you mind if I hung with you?" She asks. "I'm scared."

"Okay." She guides me back to my tent. I glance back at Laura, then up into the trees, half-expecting the woman to appear.

She doesn't.

The investigation with the class is short. Within thirty minutes, the detectives had talked to all of us to get a feel for the situation, then sent us on our way.

They obviously spent a little more time with me, but their conclusion was an animal attack. A bear, *they said.* Something large, *they said.*

A bear in Ilton? The closest thing we ever had to a bear was Big John Johnson. He had a bushy head of hair...well, let's just say he was Robin Williams with two more feet in height and ten times the amount of hair. I don't think Big John Johnson killed Laura.

I knew, but damn if I was going to tell the police that.

I didn't know it at the time, but that case would never be solved, no one would ever—

"—find out." Something rattled my arm.

"Grant, what won't we find out?" It was Mavis. "You awake?"

I slowly opened my eyes. Was there a scream? I thought I heard a scream.

"Grant, wake up."

Drowsy, *"Fuuu-uuck."*

My head pounded like a constant pendulum. I squeezed my temples, but that did nothing. "What—?"

"You were having a dream," I distantly heard Mavis say. "A bad one from what I can tell. You okay?"

I sat up and felt beads of sweat nesting in my sideburns.

"Yeah, fine. Just a nightmare."

"Wanna share?"

I looked at Mavis, wanting reassurance that if I told him, everything would be okay. He must have seen that, but instead of reassurance I got:

"You don't have to if you don't want to. If it's too personal, I'm fine with not knowing." He stood up.

"Wait," I said. So I told him. I told him all about that day and that night. I told him how it was suppose to be a great night with Laura. I was going to lose my virginity, I was going to have sex or make love…whichever because I was too young to know the difference. I told him about the daytime vision of that woman. I told him how we had fallen asleep—how *I* had fallen asleep and awoke the next morning to find that Laura had left my tent and been brutally killed.

I almost wasn't able to tell him. Near the end I welled up from the emotion, but I told him.

He came back to sit next to me and put an arm around me.

"We'll figure this thing out," he said. That was enough reassurance for me.

"I hope so."

"We have to, Grant. It's like our backs are against the wall. You have to because this thing has been terrorizing your family for years and now it's terrorizing you. I have to because this could be my only chance in my life to see one, to actually prove that one exists. We also have to so that people stop dying in your little town. Soon, you guys will have to change the population tally drastically."

I tried to muster a laugh, but as I said before, it was a long time before we laughed together. This wasn't the time the smiles would break.

After settling down, I stood.

"Mavis, I need to show you something."

CHAPTER NINE

1

How could an office look so ominous in the morning? I didn't want to go in. I didn't know how Mavis would react if I showed him the recorder, if I let him listen to it. He would think less of me, I just knew it.

I paused outside my door, trying to think of some excuse to turn around, to get him to go to *Betty's* with me. I couldn't think of anything. I had already teased him. He knew something was up and probably wouldn't let it rest until I followed through.

"You okay?" He asked.

I nodded. "Just thinking about my dreams." Weak excuse, but he let it go.

I unlocked the door and stepped in. After snapping on the lights, I waited until they completely fluttered on before moving through the middle aisle between the few desks we had.

It would be another hour before anyone arrived and that's what I hoped for. Maggie would sometimes be early, but even she liked to hit the snooze button.

"Back here," I said, guiding Mavis to my office.

He followed.

Once inside my office, I walked over to the filing cabinet. "Have a seat," I said.

He did.

I pulled the out drawer and flipped through the folders. I feared they were gone, that someone at the paper had found it. My body started to warm and I could sense my face turning red.

Then I remembered.

I reached into the very back of the drawer and pulled out the hairbrush and the tape recorder.

As I sat down, I placed them in front of Mavis.

He looked at me, then back at the items.

"I suppose you want me to ask what these are," he said.

"The hairbrush was found at the scene of the first death. Noonan's grandmother. There's still DNA on it or something. It's very old." I said all that matter-of-factly.

"I can see that it's very old," he said, "but what are you doing with it?"

"It just appeared."

"Appeared?" He reached out carefully and touched it as if it had just appeared right when I said it just appeared. It was still as solid as it was when it first appeared here. "It's real," he commented.

"I know it's real. Hamilton doesn't know it's here. It was in the evidence locker but then it wasn't. He asked me about it, but I obviously had to tell him I knew nothing about it. I think the hairbrush has something to do with my banshee friend, but exactly what I don't know." Showing him the hairbrush was the easy part of my two-part process.

"This other thing…I don't know how to explain it…" And I didn't. "Just listen."

I pressed PLAY.

He heard me ask Miss Molly what she used the recorder for. He heard her answer. His face was normal. It was normal because he didn't know what to expect.

The next part...I don't think I could listen.

"Who are you?" A pause. *"How did you get in here?"*

"That's Miss Molly," I said.

Another pause. The scream.

"Oh my God—" Then the silence.

"Where did you go..."

The doorbell rang on the tape. Hearing it a second time made it echo and I thought it was going to go on and on. The scratching

—put it in your pocket or put it in your locket, but just make sure you don't put it in a socket—

Footsteps, then an opening door.

"Oh. Hi again."

A man answered. Well, not a man, exactly. Me.

"Come in. Would you like something to drink? I have an amazing story to tell you. It just happened."

I mumbled something on the tape.

"What are you doing?" Miss Molly was getting anxious.

Quick running, then a door slammed. More scratching and then a thud. She must have thrown the recorder under the bed at this point.

I looked over at Mavis and saw him focused on the recorder. I probably could have popped him one in the nose and he wouldn't have noticed.

"What is that? What are you DOING!?" Pause. *"Grant! Stay away!"*

Mavis darted his eyes at me. I was staring right at him because I expected that to happen.

Bones cracked and then the tape shut off.

I guess it wasn't so bad letting Mavis listen to it. He was still sitting in my office, still sitting in front of me.

I caught him glancing from the recorder to me a couple of times. What did he want to say? Or worse, how did he want to accuse me? Did he want to do it outright or interrogate me?

"She said your name." He finally said. "She said 'Grant.'"

"Yes. I've already listen to it." I suppose stating the obvious wasn't necessary.

"Tell me that wasn't you."

"That wasn't me."

He eyed me. I could tell I hadn't convinced him. "You sure? Your name…" Mavis was just as confused as I was when I had first heard it.

"I really can't positively say that it was or wasn't me. My name is mentioned sure, but I have no clue why I went back to Miss Molly's or when or how." I leaned back. "Sorry, I'm just not sure."

"Do you have any periods of time that you can't remember? Like you just woke up from something?"

I shook my head. "Just my normal sleeping."

"Hmm-hmmm."

"What?" I snapped. For a second I thought I had Bobby in my office.

"Just thinking," he said.

I grabbed the hairbrush and the recorder and slid them back into the drawer.

Mavis turned in his seat. "Does Hamilton know about that tape recorder?"

"No. That's why it's here."

"Well, keep it here. Better yet, you should find a different place to hide it and the brush. Somewhere you only know about and could never be found by someone like Hamilton."

"Okay,"

"And don't tell me, either."

2

I watched Mavis leave my office, then exit the front door. He "had to mull this over". Mull this over
—mull it right out of town—
And get back to me with some research. I didn't know what kind of research he was expecting to do, but I knew he just needed to get away from me for a bit. Like we were two brothers who had just had a big fight and mom told us to separate and cool down.

Yeah, that's what Mavis was doing. Cooling off.

What else was he suppose to do? He just possibly heard me on tape killing Miss Molly. There's an old hairbrush from one of the crime scenes sitting on my desk. What else was he suppose to think and do? I would probably do the same thing.

Cool off.

I leaned back in my chair and drifted off. Half wishing when I woke up, all this would go away.

3

Heels clicking on the floor startled me awake. I eased up and checked my watch. I was out for about thirty minutes. I looked out into the main office and saw Maggie strolling in. She flipped on the lights and they vibrated to life.

I stood. My chair creaked against the floor.

"Grant?" Maggie's sweet voice floated in.

"Yeah, I'm here."

"What are you doing here so early?"

I shrugged. What to tell her. I was rarely here this early, so she had every right to be a little curious.

"I had some stuff to take care of," I said.

"Stuff? What kind of stuff?"

"Just thinking. Stuff."

"Does it have anything to do with that man that's been hanging around town?"

"What?"

"Come on, Grant. I'm in the newspaper business. Do you think my eyes don't work?"

"Maybe, maybe not. It doesn't matter."

"It does if it's affecting you."

I hung out in the doorway and searched for something on Maggie's face that would indicate the end of the interrogation, but she was 1) a woman and 2) aware that something was up. When Maggie knew something was up she usually didn't let up.

"Look," she said. "I don't know what is going on. I don't know what is making you sneak around town with some strange-looking man who many people think might stir up some trouble, but whatever it is, Grant, you know that I am your friend."

Was I getting off that easy?

"Grant? Do you know?"

"Yes, I do."

"Promise me that you'll come to me if you need to talk."

I smiled. "You being sincere or do you just want a story?"

At least she heard my tone. "Well, if I do get a story, I'd want it published in a real paper. Not this rag."

She came around my desk and gave me a peck on the cheek. "I'm here if you need me. There's nothing that would shock me. Promise me you'll talk to me if you need to."

Maggie paused. If she wanted me to spill it all now, she wasn't going to get it.

And saying *there's nothing that would shock me*? Did she actually know something? She was a pretty open gal...in many things...but I believed what I could tell her would shock her.

"Maggie, you're my gal."

"Okay."

I stood. "I need some coffee."

"I could make you some."

"Maybe I should rephrase that: I need some *good* coffee." I guided Maggie from my office. "I'll be at *Betty's* if you need me."

4

A good pick-me-up came from *Betty's* if you asked for the special sauce. Sounds dirty, but her dark coffee went down thick, but somehow quickly got into your bloodstream to revive everything about you. Betty said that it's just a placebo kinda thing. It's probably a caffeine kinda thing.

As I walked through the paper's door, I saw Bobby leaning against his patrol car. When he saw me, he popped his hand up in a short wave.

"Hey," he said.

"Hey, Bobby," I slowed my walking, but continued on.

"Where you headed?"

"*Betty's.* I need some coffee."

"That so?"

"Yup, that's so."

"How about if I owe you that coffee," he said.

"Owe me? Why?" I stopped and turned. He was less than a foot behind me and forced himself not to run into me.

"Get in the car."

"You got any candy for me?" I mocked.

"Fuck you, Grant. Just get in the car."

"I don't think so. Tell me what's up first." I restarted my walking.

I could hear his damn cop feet plodding along the sidewalk. "Stop Goddamn it! I need you to get in the car!"

Once again I stopped and turned towards him. I didn't say anything, but when I saw his eyes, I knew that there was something he did need me to get in the car for.

It wasn't to kidnap me or take me down to the station, I sensed. It was something more.

"Fine," I said.

Relieved, Bobby jogged to the police car.

When we got into the car, he said, "Thank you."

He pulled out into the street and gunned the accelerator. When we had gone a couple of blocks, he reached down and flipped on the sirens. The wail startled Megan, who worked as a clerk at the grocery store.

I hoped she didn't think I was being taken in. Hell, I hope I wasn't being taken in.

5

When we left the Ilton town limits, I peered over at Bobby. "So…where are we going?"

Bobby turned off the siren.

"Out of town."

I laughed. "I figured that Einstein. But *where?*"

He slowed the car a little.

"Look, Grant," he said. "Let's get a few things out on the table."

"I thought the table was clear."

He chuckled. "Right. That table hasn't been clear since high school."

"Why are we like this?" I asked. "I sometimes wonder how you and I got to this point."

"I don't know how, but let's not get *Lifetime* on each other." He blew a stop sign—the only one within five miles, I'm sure—then sped up. "We rarely see eye to eye and I understand this. I'm the police chief and you're the town journalist. Maybe we are supposed to have a rivalry, who knows. What I do know is that we always seem to be at each other's throats and that's not what this town needs. Especially now. Got me so far?"

"Sure, sure." Where was he going with this?

"As far as our jobs go, I think we enjoy what we do. You get under my skin and I get under your skin—"

I laughed. "Two of the best understatements of the decade."

I caught the hardass smiling.

"Don't lie to yourself. I know I get under your skin. I've seen how you look when I'm in your presence."

"Okay, okay. You bug me. I agree."

"I just want us to get along now, to get this whole thing solved. I feel this town is my child and I don't want to see my child hurt. I honestly think that you and I are the best people to figure this thing out."

"I see. How do you think I can be involved?"

"You're already involved." He didn't say anything right after and I wondered if he knew about my own personal evidence locker.

"I know you've been doing some research on your own. You brought that weird guy into town, didn't you?"

"Yes."

"Will you tell me about him?"

"Not at the moment."

"Fine." He sounded like he didn't expect that answer and had no further questioning for me.

Boy was I wrong.

Another turn later, Bobby brought out the big questions.

"So," he murmured. "What do you think about Maggie?"

I turned my body toward him, wondering where the hell that question came from.

"She's a great employee," I quickly replied. Any longer of a pause and things would have gotten interesting, I'm sure.

"You fuckin' well know that's not what I meant."

"Well, she is. I don't know what other respect you mean."

Bobby laughed. "Don't get journalistic on me, Grant. I know you like her."

"Like her? Sure, I do. We've worked together for a long time. We've talk about many things—"

"So what you're saying is that you two have a history?"

"I guess you can say that."

"And where does that history end?"

"Just what kind of history do you think we had?"

Bobby paused. I saw him glance at me. Did he not expect any questions in return?

"I think you've had a close history and you are trying to keep that history going," he said.

"You'd be so far from the truth if you think that."

"Mmm-hmm."

Oh yes. There it was. That's the Bobby I was used to.

"Disbelieving?" I countered.

"Yes."

"Okay. Don't believe me, I don't care." I checked my watch. "Take me back to town."

"I am in love with Maggie, so don't wreck that," Bobby said. "I know you still have feelings for her, but I don't want to see those feelings realized."

"No feelings. No more history. Bobby, you can just drop it."

"I hope this is the end of this conversation."

"No problem."

But my mind continued the conversation. My mind and my heart told each other how much I missed Maggie.

How much I wanted to hold her, lie next to her in bed, take her to the movies, do all that dating shit all over again. My mind reminded my heart how much it yearned for her.

Thanks, mind.

"What's wrong?" Bobby asked.

"Nothing. Just wondering where the hell you're taking me."

"There," he said, pointing ahead of him.

6

"This happened twenty or so minutes ago," Bobby continued. He slowed the car as we approached.

Ahead of us, multiple police cars (from county of course), fire engines, and ambulances sat in haphazard fashion on both sides of the road. Men from the respective municipals milled around the scene waiting for instruction.

A few men huddled around one part of the scene. Near them was an overturned car, its front end a horrendous mess of metal and bridge railing.

"What happened?" I asked.

"Don't know how the car got like that, but we do know what happened to the driver." Bobby stopped the car at the back end of the crowd of cars. "Let's go."

I didn't understand why I was here right now. I didn't understand the drive over and I didn't understand the conversation about Maggie. The only thing I did understand was that I couldn't even *think* about Maggie and Bobby would have my hide.

I followed Bobby through the maze of cops and detectives. He was stopped only once and Bobby had to remind that person that this was his county and as of this moment, this was his crime scene.

Oddly enough, not one of Bobby's deputies was in the vicinity, so that didn't make sense.

"So where's the driver?" I asked.

"Over there."

He motioned away from the car. "By the bridge." He switched directions.

I followed Bobby around a county police car. Ahead, I saw a leg draped over the guard rail. I slowed. There was something familiar about the leg. Not the leg, but the pants. Khaki pants. Dockers, to be exact. I didn't know how I knew that those exact pants on that exact victim were Dockers. But only one person I knew wore Dockers.

"No." I stopped.

Bobby looked back and gave me a look of sympathy. "You have to," he said. Or at least that's what I thought he said.

"No."

"Grant," Bobby said matter-of-factly, "it's Pete."

Whether it took Bobby to actually say it or whether I knew in the back of his mind, my legs buckled and I almost went cascading to the ground.

A few of the counties gave me their attention for a moment, but there was no caring in the glances. They returned to their previous task of surveying the accident scene.

"Don't embarrass me in front of the County assholes." A smile formed on Bobby's face, but I couldn't muster a response. It was a joke, I knew, but I barely heard it.

I regained my footing and slowly made my way over to the guardrail.

"It's just an accident, right?" I asked.

"No. It was no accident."

"What? Looks like one to me." My voice was returning.

"I'll show you why. No accident happens like this."

"Why?"

"Pete was beaten to death."

7

I cautiously strolled to the guardrail, not particularly wanting to see what Pete looked like. Who would? I only looked for Bobby's sake. Who the fuck was I kidding? I had to see. I needed to see.

Besides the pants, I also recognized Pete's shoes. He dressed casual in his shirts and pants, but sporty in his sneakers. His Nike's were white, with mesh netting on the top of the foot to air it out when things got a little smelly and sweaty. The Nike Swoosh was red. An untied right shoe hung over the metal rail, dangling to its last moments of being a shoe. The shoe was probably cast aside as he was thrown from the car.

I looked back at the car, which was at least three hundred feet away. Pete had been thrown pretty far.

"He was thrown?" I asked.

Bobby only shook his head.

"Then what?"

"I want you to see him first." Bobby stayed planted in his spot. Hell, he already had a good look…now it was my turn.

I reached the rail and could immediately tell that his leg was twisted in ways I've never seen before. It was bent, but also twisted at the knee and hip. Blood soaked the other shoe and the foot angled weirdly, as if someone was trying to learn about right angles.

My eyes moved up.

Pete's shirt had managed to expose his stomach and sides. There, large bruises inhabited most of the stomach and welts the size of tennis balls protruded grossly. Any minute they looked like they were going to pop.

"Oh God, Pete," I murmured.

Nothing was left of Pete's face. Maybe a left check. Other than that, someone had ripped the flesh of his face away. Blood dripped onto the ground in glue-like teardrops. The whites of Pete's eyes poked out like some grotesque skeleton in the beginning stages of becoming a skeleton.

I turned.

I puked on the side of the road.

I felt Bobby approach and I wiped my mouth and regained my composure back.

"I'm pretty sure he was beaten," Bobby said.

"Beaten? How can you tell?" I asked.

"Simply by the marks," Bobby said. "He was not thrown from the car. My guess is he was in the car as it rolled over and landed like it did. Whoever beat him *pulled* him from the car and dragged him over here, did the business, and left him for dead—" Bobby caught the last part of his statement and corrected it with "—left him here."

Bobby pointed to the marks on Pete's face. "Those are not car accident marks," he said. "Those are marks of someone who had it in for him."

"Pete didn't have any enemies. I don't understand who would do this," I said.

"No one has any enemies they know of. That's what makes them enemies."

"But around here? What kind of enemy could Pete have?"

Bobby sighed. "I don't know, but from the looks of the wounds, someone used a blunt object and really put it to him. A lot of force."

I have to admit, Bobby sounded pretty convincing. Blunt object, wounds, marks: good old Chief Hamilton was looking at this death with sharp eyes.

Some static erupted from Bobby's walkie.

I pointed to Pete. "Mind if I have a closer look?"

Bobby glanced at the scene and back at the county cops. "Sure. Just don't let them see you. This scene won't be mine too much longer."

I nodded. When he turned to answer the call, I eased myself over the guardrail and knelt down next to Pete.

"Pete, Pete. What happened here," I whispered.

The body was getting easier to look at, but blood continued to spill onto the ground. My shoes were inches from a pool that started to form and I scooted back. As I did, I saw it.

Near Pete's ear was a thin stick. The closer I looked, the more I realized that it was plastic. On one end was a knob. It looked like a cane for a miniature guy.

But I knew what it was. I didn't have to pick it up to know it was a hairbrush bristle.

Worse, it looked like it came from the bane sitting in my file cabinet. That fucking, hidden silver hairbrush.

I couldn't let it stay.

I heard Bobby still speaking into his walkie and rolled my eyes to the right. His back was still turned. With one swift motion, I swung my hand down and scooped up the bristle. Dirt and rock came with it, but as long as I got the evidence, I was good.

As I stood, I dropped everything from my hand into my pocket. Footsteps approached from behind me.

"Anything?" It was Bobby.

"Nah, sorry. Can we go?"

"Not yet. I want to ask you a couple of questions."

"What, like a suspect?"

"No, like someone who knew Pete."

I felt uneasy about this, but I said, "Fine, go ahead."

"When was the last time you saw Pete?" Just get right into it, why don't you, Bobby.

"Yesterday. At work."

"What time?"

"The morning."

"Not in the afternoon?"

"If I did I would have said." This did not amuse Bobby. "I took the afternoon off."

"On Tuesday?"

"Yes, on Tuesday."

"I see." He removed a pad from his shirt pocket and jotted something down. "What did you do?"

Was he serious? "What do you mean 'what did I do'? Why are you asking me this question?"

"I need to place you somewhere away from Pete. If I can't do it, you need to help me out." Bobby poised the pen over the pad, but I kept silent.

"Nothing?" He finally asked.

"I would like to go, please." I said.

Bobby took a step forward. He removed an object from his pocket. "Is this yours?"

I averted my eyes down. It was my flash drive from the office. A titanium Sandisk drive that I kept all my editorials and articles on. How the fuck did he get it?

"Yes," I said, resigned.

"I thought so," Bobby said, confident.

"Where did you find it?"

"Where do you think?"

I felt Bobby's stare as I stared at the flash drive. I shrugged. "I thought it was sitting on my desk."

"It wasn't. I found it in Pete's pocket."

"What? I have no idea how it got there." I really didn't, but I realized by saying that, I probably sounded guiltier. I thought back to the past few days. Come to think of it, I really didn't speak to Pete a lot. Maybe a hello here and there, but I pretty much let him do what he wanted.

Did I let him borrow my flash drive? I don't see why he would need it. It's just my editorials and my own articles.

"I must have let him borrow it."

"If so, do you remember when?" he asked.

"I'm not even sure if I did!"

Bobby stood silent. I didn't know what to say. I didn't know what he wanted to hear because there is no explanation in any world or in the universe that I could give that would appease Bobby.

"Look, I used my flash drive last night for a few moments. I must have left it on my desk and he grabbed it for some reason. That reason I don't know." I hoped that would help, but apparently it didn't.

"So what is on the flash drive?"

"My editorials and some of my articles," I answered.

"Is that all?"

What did he mean by 'is that all'? It was only for work and that's all I saved on there. There are probably over a hundred editorials and articles. So yeah, that was all.

"Yeah, just documents," I finally answered.

"Nothing else?"

"Just fucking say it!" I screamed. The counties turned to look at me again.

Bobby latched onto my arm. He had a pretty tight grip. I felt the blood pump through my muscle, throbbing because of the small space the blood was being allowed to flow through.

"Don't you fucking scream out here. I will drop you in a heartbeat." He gave me a little shove towards his squad car. "Get in there."

Now this was a change of attitude. Nice Mr. Bobby Hamilton bringing me along for a ride, chatting me up like I was his friend. And this. And this implied attitude that I killed Pete. I know Bobby looked at me with contempt. I know he thought I killed Pete, but there must be something deep down within that asshole that knows I didn't kill him. Sure we hated each other, but we weren't stupid.

I sat in the passenger seat. "In the front, right?" I tried a joke to see where we stood.

He said nothing. We stood bad.

Bobby sat in his seat and plugged the flash drive into his police computer. After a moment, a window appeared that showed my files.

But there were other files that I was unfamiliar with below my documents. They looked like they were .JPG files. Pictures.

"What are those?" I asked.

"Pictures. There are pictures on your flash drive."

"Pictures of what?"

He clicked the first one and it opened.

The picture was of Miss Molly's house, time unknown. Bobby closed that one and opened up the second one. This time the picture was closer to the house, but a figure could be seen on the front lawn. The figure appeared to be just standing there.

"Did Pete take these?" I asked.

"I don't know," he said. "My guess is yes and whoever beat him up, wanted this flash drive."

"You think that was me," I said nonchalantly.

He didn't deny it, but said, "My other guess is that someone else took these pictures and gave them to Pete."

Bobby pulled up another picture. The figure had moved along and was opening the front door. He didn't stay on that picture too long before loading up another one.

The last picture chilled me.

Two figures darkened the curtain, which I suspected was in Miss Molly's bedroom. One of the figures was Miss Molly; I could make out her form, but the other I couldn't recognize.

"Is that Miss Molly?" I asked.

Bobby nodded.

"And the other?"

Bobby closed the picture and shut the lid of his laptop. "I think the other is you."

8

As we pulled away from the accident, the county police eased up to either side of the road as we passed them. The driver of the one on our left gave Bobby a nod. Ilton's Chief of Police obliged and even supplied a wave in return.

"Assholes," he said.

Well, I thought, that's exactly how I felt about you. Especially in the past hour or so. My feelings were actually becoming amiable until he decided to accuse me of killing Miss Molly.

Asshole, indeed.

"I hope that's not you in the picture, Grant."

I kept my eyes out my window.

"But who else could it be?" he asked, softly, so it sounded more like he asked himself.

"How can you even recognize me?" I asked calmly.

"Your silhouette."

"That's shit and you know it. It's a picture. There's barely a silhouette."

"Perhaps."

Silhouette? The damn picture was taken too far away to determine anyone's silhouette. It could have been

Jack the Ripper's silhouette and Hamilton would have thought it was me.

"Take me back to town," I mumbled.

"Sure," Bobby said. "Want a copy of the pictures? Do your own investigation?"

"I should ask you if *you* want a copy of the pictures. It's my flash drive."

"Evidence. I am obliged to keep it"

"You are obliged to do shit." I planted my eyes back out the window. "Town."

9

Bobby stopped in front of the newspaper building. Before I got out I turned to him and said, "Think about this for a moment: if I killed Pete for the flash drive, why was it still left on him?"

"Out," was his answer.

I got out and watched him go.

"Prick," I said.

He poked his hand out of the squad car's window as if he heard me and gave me a one-motion wave. It wasn't even a friendly wave. Just something you gave your boss or that guy who lived down the street that you kind of hated, but you really didn't know him. He just walked funny and never picked up the trash if the can got knocked over.

"Grant," I heard behind me.

I turned and Maggie stood a few feet from me.

"Where have you been, Grant?"

"Out of town."

"Funny. Were you with Bobby?"

"Yup. He nabbed me and took me on a nice picnic. I told him it should have been you, but he insisted." My humor was lost on her face. Her lips turned inward into a scowl.

"Did he take you to see the accident?" She asked flatly.

That news traveled fast. Hell, I was only gone for a short time. "How did you know so quickly?"

"I know some county people," she answered.

"Well, don't you have the little network. You probably don't want to tell Bobby that." I paused. A little harsh, probably. "Look, I'm sorry, I'm just a bit stressed right now. Bobby did take me out there. He asked me not to talk about it."

"Can you say anything about it at all?"

"It was horrible. I don't understand how something like this could happen. To Pete of all people."

Maggie nodded. "It was just an accident. Things happen. Who knows? He swerved to miss an animal or hit a bump the wrong way."

"Yeah, I guess."

"Why don't you go and relax. Get in some napping. I know how you like those naps." She took my arm in hers and guided me down the sidewalk. "I'll close up shop here."

"Okay," I said. That was a good idea.

After a half of block of

—hand in hand holding her soft palm and fingers curling into mine—

strolling along she broke away.

"I'll call you later," she said.

"Okay," was all I said.

And I headed home to relax.

10

My brother was Johnathon. With an 'H'. The spelling of his name always confused teachers. My mother and father told us that some of the first people to settle America were ancestors and that some of them were named Johnathon with an 'H'. My brother was always quick to inform the teachers of this fact when he sensed their confusion. After that he made them call him by the full name. I was the only one that could call him John.

John was exactly one year younger than me to the day. We looked alike so it was very easy for everyone to tell we were brothers. The only difference was that he had blonde hair and I had black hair. Other than that we could have been twins and sometimes we were mistaken for one another. Occasionally we took advantage of this but we knew when it was inappropriate.

When I was eleven, we decided to do some exploring one day. The tiny forest next to our house was always ripe for adventure, or so we liked to believe. We camped there often but we mainly liked to explore. There was a small section near the back of the forest that we had never gone to before and that day, John was hell-bent on going. I would never know why.

And I do mean never.

"Grant, let's go," he said as we stepped from the creek to the shore. He was already up the embankment facing me with his hands on his hips. "I want to get there before dark."

"Carry something then!" I had our tent, food, extra clothes, toiletries and whatever else he packed in the duffle bag.

John grunted and headed off out of view. No sense in calling after him: once he got it in his head to do something there was nothing I could do. I was the same way just a year ago and I'm sure he said the same about me.

I finally managed to reach the top of the bank and stopped to catch my breath. I couldn't see my brother anywhere and called him a few bad names my eleven-year-old mind knew. Nothing harsh just a few minor ones out of annoyance.

"John!" I yelled out.

No answer. He must really want to get to the back part bad. "John!" But still nothing. He definitely could hear me. This forest wasn't that big. Sometimes on a quiet night when we were camping we could hear our mom washing dishes. The clinks of the plates filtering out like mosquitoes. You knew they were there; you just couldn't see them.

I was tired. I couldn't wait to get the fire started. John would have to pitch the tent while I prepared dinner. He'd have no choice because I was going to make him. I pictured him throwing a fuss, but I knew how to thwart it.

"John!" Damn him. Where was he? He wasn't one to play a joke like this. I wonder if he went back home for some reason. John always had a problem peeing outdoors. Loved camping, but hated going to the bathroom outdoors. Strange boy sometimes, but he was my brother and—

"Grant! Help! Helll—!"

His voice cut off. I whipped my head to the left.

"John! Where are you?!"

Nothing. I dropped the bags and tent and started sprinting in the direction of the voice. I hoped it was the right direction. With all these trees, the sound could bounce around and come from anywhere. It was a guess, but I thought his scream came from the back of the forest, where we wanted to camp tonight.

I leapt over a fallen tree and through some brush. I felt branches and thorns grab at me and attempt to slow me down, but John's voice sounded desperate. Like he was escaping from something.

How far was this place? I bounded over something that actually looked like a path. A well-worn path. What was it doing here? This was private property. Not a community state park.

And then I tripped.

I arced towards the ground at horrible speed. I didn't even have time to get my hands out in front of me to help with the impact. The ground slammed into my body hard. Immediate pain raced through my bones at a breakneck pace and I had barely enough time to do a body check when I looked up through a set of trees and saw John's legs.

With another pair of legs.

John was being dragged.

11

I jerked awake, confused. I focused my eyes on my surroundings and remembered I had come home to take a nap. Come home to get away from all the bad things.

No amount of coming home will get all the weight that seemed to be pressing down on this town.

Pressing down on me.

CHAPTER TEN

1

A quick shower didn't help. Just got myself clean and smelling less like the killer Bobby thought I was. The shower felt nice, but the world did not lift from my shoulders or the death surrounding me did not disappear when I turned off the faucets. Stop the flow of water, stop the flow of death: that's how it should work.

Damn, I was becoming a sad sack tonight.

My cordless chimed its happy ring and I snatched it.

"Hello?" I said.

It was Maggie. A nice surprise to say the least. This should be interesting.

"What's up?" Not the coolest sounding phrase, but I was a bit nervous: she rarely called me out of the blue since we broke up. For work things, sure, but nothing more.

"Hey Grant. How are you?"

"Fine. Just got out of the shower. Looking to get in a relaxing night." This was *not* shaping up to be an interesting conversation.

"Yeah. That sounds good." A pause. *Get to it, Maggie. Why the call?*

"Well," she continued, "I wanted to see how you were and if you needed anything."

"Not really." I said. "I'm just going to hit the mattress."

"But it's only 7:30."

I hadn't realized it was so early. Nap, shower, thoughts of me killing half the town: I figured it was well past ten. "I suppose I won't go to bed then," I said.

"Have you eaten?"

"No."

"You have to eat something. Why don't I come over and make you something?" She chuckled. "You got food in that place right?"

"Of course!" Of course I wanted her to come over. Real bad. At least if I said yes, I couldn't be the bad guy or the creep. She asked me, so there it was then. Like old times and all that. I badly wanted to feel her arm caressing my chest as we laid in bed after a great session of lovemaking. Lovemaking? That sounded too romantic. Sex. Great session of sex. "Sure. If you want. No plans with Bobby?"

I tried to stop the question but it was out.

"He's got the night shift." Hmm...no acknowledgement. This could work to my advantage.

I really missed her.

"Great. I'll be over in few," she said. "Bye."

Before I could say anything, the dial tone confronted me. I gently laid the handset in the cradle and looked around my place.

Time to do the bachelor clean-up. Hopefully there was enough room in my closet to shove my mess.

A few minutes meant twenty. The doorbell rang and I tossed the last of my paper dishes in the trash and gave the apartment one last look-over. Not bad. It's habitable so we would survive.

My stomach flipped and my heart raced a little more than normal. Was it because of Maggie? This was not high school nor was this a first date. Maggie and I have done some things that high-schoolers only wished they could dream about and that people on first dates didn't do until...well, maybe they never did those things Maggie and I did. I blossomed sexually with Maggie. So why was I nervous?

The answer sat in that part of the brain you reserved for answers to questions you didn't want to admit.

The doorbell rang again and I realized Maggie stood out there. What a jackass host.

I ran to the door and slung it open.

"Hi!" I said, my voice cracking. "I was upstairs."

"Hey, Grant."

She walked in without an invitation, which was fine by me. As she strolled by, I saw a tote from our local grocery store.

"What's in the bag?" I asked.

She whirled. Her hair fanned out and it was followed with a large smile. I thought of going to her and giving her a kiss right there, to show her that I

—love you love you love you—

still had some feelings for her. Just for her information. A little FYI for her heart.

"Well, I stopped off by the store just in case you were light on food and picked up some spaghetti and chicken and a little Alfredo sauce."

"Sounds wonderful." It did.

"Yeah. Like I said, you have to eat."

Maggie went into the kitchen and within seconds I heard pots and pans rattling and my silverware drawer opening. She still knew her way around my place and I just stood in the living room listening to her sounds, picturing her floating

—screaming bitch death teeth sticks of death—

Her arms and hands seductively turned the knobs on the stove and prepared the chicken. Her soft hands gripped the knife with a purpose. She didn't grasp the handle tight; this I knew from when she held my hands and…well, other parts. Maggie would hold it just right where I knew she was there and could move me in ways no one would ever move me in a lifetime. Not too soft, not to tight.

Just perfect.

"Whatchya doing in there?" I heard her call.

"TV."

"I don't hear it."

I grabbed the remote and quickly turned on the TV to whatever channel was on. Great, PBS. And a special about monkeys, no less.

Maggie popped out and glanced at the TV. She was wiping her hands. "Monkeys? Really?"

I shrugged.

"Got the chicken cut. About ten minutes?"

"Sure, sure. I'm going to go wash up."

She chuckled. "Okay." Maggie returned to the kitchen.

I bounded up the stairs and rushed to the bathroom. After shutting the door, I took a few minutes to catch my breath and relax.

She's with Bobby Hamilton. What chance did I have to reclaim my previous love with her? *But she is downstairs cooking me dinner in my own house*

—he's got the night shift—

So that's got to be something.

But it wasn't and I knew this.

3

Back downstairs, Maggie placed plates of food on my table. Steam rose and quickly disappeared and second later, I could smell the spaghetti and suddenly, I was hungry.

"It's all ready," she said.

"Smell's wonderful."

"Basic. You can't really fuck up pasta." She sat down.

I followed and helped myself to a heaping pile of spaghetti.

"Listen," Maggie began, "let's talk."

I set my fork down. Looks like I really wasn't going to enjoy this. "What's up?"

"Well, what's going on with you?"

"Just getting right into it, eh?" I wasn't hungry anymore. I pushed the plate back, took a sip of my Heineken, and sighed.

"Yes I am. You've been acting really strange. I know what people are saying. I know what the rumors are. Do I believe it? I don't know. The way you've been walking around this town, all quiet, all reserved, I don't know what to think."

I shrugged. "I've just had some things going on."

"Yeah, you've said that already. Talk to me." Her voice lowered on the last sentence. This was when Maggie got serious and I knew she wasn't going to let me off the hook. It didn't matter how many excuses I threw at her or how much I stalled, Maggie was not going to set me free. If anything, she would call me out.

She continued. "It's not the paper. Hell, when you think about it, the rest of us there do all your work. You throw in an editorial once in a while, but you have a staff of writers, an adman to sell space, and a printer. Besides not getting laid, you need to explain yourself."

"We could perhaps fix that part." I winked at her, but it was too far when she was full mode serious.

"Not funny. Quit stalling."

I stared at her eyes.

What should I say? How much should I say? I really wanted to say nothing, but that would not happen. Obviously I couldn't say everything. Pick and choose I guess.

"Having a little trouble starting? That's what your eyes are saying." She smirked. "Why don't you start with your new friend?"

"His name is Mavis."

"Don't get offended. Start with him."

"He's a ghosthunter."

"Yeah, you definitely need to start with him, then."

I laughed and she followed suit. It felt good to laugh with her. "He is helping me find a ghost that has haunted my family for generations."

"What? That's sounds a little bit crazy. You never told me this before."

"I know, I know. Do you believe in ghosts?"

She shook her head. "No. No offense to Mavis, but I don't."

"No harm. I've been seeing this ghost a lot over the past few years—" The first lie. "—and I don't know why she has appeared again."

"She?"

"Yes. The ghost is a she."

"Is she hot?" Maggie was starting to crack jokes. Maybe she wasn't really interested in my story which I would love, but I wanted to continue.

"I guess. In an old folksy way. Anyway, I've been having horrible dreams about her killing my family and I've been having them about twice a week lately."

"Wait. Dreams? Have you seen this ghost in real life?"

"Yes.

"Hmmm."

"Hmmm? Is that all you have to say to that?"

"Sure is. I don't believe in them."

"That means you don't believe me."

"No. I believe that *you* believe."

The clock ticked slowly. How much more did I have to endure with Maggie? If she didn't believe me, why listen? Tonight seemed like there was no point.

But I continued anyway. "I don't know why the dreams are affecting me so much, but they just are."

She shook her head. "This has nothing to do about the dreams. Did you ask Mavis to be here?"

I nodded.

"And about what Bobby?"

I laughed. "What about him? You're fucking him, what more is there to know."

"This has nothing to do with that either. Why has he been around to see you so much?"

"Maybe he likes my company more than yours?"

"Get serious!" Maggie slammed her hand on the table. Frustration. "Hiding it from me will only make it worse when I find out what is really going on."

"What have you heard?"

"That you killed Noonan, Molly, and Betty."

"Yup. I heard that to."

I knew she wanted to ask me if I did. She wanted to hear it from me, but I wasn't going to say anything unless she asked. I knew she wasn't going to ask and that was or wasn't her prerogative. She should have the answer already. She knew me.

"Have you now. Is that why Bobby's been on your ass every day?"

"Maybe. Doesn't matter. He's got his life and I've got mine. He just wants me to keep it out of the paper until he has definite information about everything."

"Sure." I knew she wasn't swallowing it, but she was finally going to let it go. "Well, I hope you enjoyed your dinner."

"What I had of it, I did."

She stuck her finger in the food in the plate. "It's still warm. Finish it up."

"Yeah, sure." But I wasn't. I wanted her out of my house more than I wanted her in my house earlier. Maggie stood.

"I should go."

To be nice: "Are you sure? You can stay here. Watch a movie or something if you want since your beau's on the night shift."

"Thanks for the offer, but no. It would be wrong."

"Would it? We can just be friends. You know how to be that don't you?"

"Fuck you, Grant. You can't act the way you did when we were together and assume that we can just be friends."

"Why can't I think that after it's been so long?"

She walked towards the door. "You became distant then and you continue to be distant now. Friends aren't like that."

"Right. Please leave."

"Fine," she said.

Without another word, she let herself out. I crept to the window and looked out. I watched her get into her car and leave.

So much for a night of wild and unlawful sex.

I woke up the next morning with a headache that traveled around my head like someone broke a bottle inside my brain and the shards were bouncing from one side of the skull to the other side in seconds.

Vaguely, I recalled a very sad night of arguing with Maggie and losing her just a little more as a friend.

I slipped from the bed and made my way to the bathroom. On the way, I noticed that the clock read 1:30 p.m. Afternoon?

The phone rang.

Daryl. "Hey Grant. You coming in today?"

"No," I said. "Not feeling too well."

"You okay?"

"I should be fine after the weekend. I just need to relax. Bad headache. I feel like puking."

"Get better. Anything you want me to concentrate on?"

"Nah. Why don't you take the rest of the afternoon off and enjoy the weekend. Tell the others to do the same."

"You sure?"

"Yeah," I said. "Why not? I'm taking one. You guys do the same."

"But you're sick."

"Never heard anyone complain about a free three-day weekend."

He laughed. "Okay boss, will do."

"See you later."

I hung up and sat back down on the bed. My headache. Where did this come from?

Almost immediately, the phone rang again.

"Fuck!"

I picked it up again, almost dropping the handset from grabbing it too hard. "Hello?"

"Grant?"

"Yeah, what's up? Who's this?"

"Mavis."

"Oh hey. Find anything new?"

"No," he said. "Been trying. Checking out the town. Attempting to talk to the townspeople."

I laughed.

"What?" he asked.

"Do people say townspeople anymore? You from the 1800's?"

"I know, I know." I heard a little chuckle on his end. "I go to a lot of old Nordic and Scottish places that still have that mentality."

"I see."

"The people of Ilton aren't very talkative, are they?"

"Not really. Not to strangers. And especially not to you, I imagine."

"I understand."

"Yeah. It seems like I'm a stranger to them lately."

"I'm trying to change that."

"I know."

"What are you doing now?"

I didn't know. I really didn't know. "Nothing, really. Probably just going to nap. I've got a terrible headache."

"Why don't you come out with me? Check some things out."

I thought about it for a second. "Nah, that's okay."

"You sure? You don't sound so good," he said matter-of-factly.

"I'm just tired."

"Okay."

There was that awkward pause where no one knows if this was the end of the conversation. Mavis and I both hung on for a few seconds in silence.

"Why don't I bring a six-pack over and we can polish it off. Just relax," he offered.

"Maybe," I said.

"Talk to you later then."

I hung up the phone and prayed nobody else was in the mood to cheer me up.

5

I napped again. I woke exhausted more than before and with a headache that was still there. I quickly went to the answering machine and there were no messages. The caller I.D. showed no missed calls, so apparently no one else was concerned about me.

That was good.

Then, as if on cue, like someone was writing my life in screenplay form, decided *"hey, let's do something ironic. Because our character is annoyed that people continue to call him, let's take it one step further and have someone appear at their door."*

Yeah, really funny, screenwriter.

I went to the door anyway and saw Mavis there when I opened it. He was holding a six-pack. He proffered it to me. "Thought I'd just show up."

Defeated, I stepped back and motioned for him to come through. Mavis did and went to the kitchen. I immediately heard drawers opening and then, "You got a bottle opener?"

I shook my head. This was just like last night except I didn't plan on having sex with Mavis.

"Yeah, be there in a second."

As I shut the door, I caught a glimpse of Bobby creeping by in his cruiser. When he passed my house, he sped up slightly and I waited until he was around the corner before completely shutting the door.

I joined Mavis in the kitchen, found my bottle opener and had a beer in my hand before anything else was said.

"So you like being holed up in your house all day?" He asked.

"Why not? No one bothers you—" I pointed to Mavis. "Well, some don't and you can eat what you want and no one suspects that you killed anybody."

"I guess. But if there's something needing to be done, then how can you do it in here?"

He had a good way of thinking about things.

"I know you're having a hard time right now," he said, "but sitting in here isn't going to figure things out."

"That's why I asked you to come here."

"I can't find these ghosts on my own." Mavis took a swig of beer. "They are connected to you in some way."

"They? You think there's more than one?"

"Well, they are very busy. How could just one be haunting you and other parts of this town?"

"I can't believe that there are ghosts in this town."

Mavis laughed. "How strange you say that when one is bugging the shit out of you!" He got serious. "Don't you believe in ghosts?"

I shrugged. "I have to do I?"

"Not that you have to, but you should."

I shook my head. "And why is that?"

CHAPTER ELEVEN

1

"It was in Germany, twent-five years ago," Mavis began. "I was ten or eleven at the time. My age doesn't matter; I was a kid. I changed from then on."

2

Mavis's father, William, was already staying at the old, sixty-seven room castle in Germany when Mavis and his mother arrived on a cold and damp Saturday morning.

The surrounding hills pushed up light patches of fog, which hovered unmoving. The castle grounds made a heavy green perimeter going three hundred yards in each direction. At the edge of the lawn, massive trees blocked any view into the horizon.

Nighttime would be creepy, Mavis thought.

A vacation for his dad included investigating a series of hauntings at an old castle. Hence, *this* investigation at *this* castle. He wanted Mavis and his mom Rebecca to join him because they haven't had a proper vacation as a family in over five years. The last time included a tour of Asia: Japan, Korea and parts of China. The Great Wall impressed Mavis the most, but in all three countries, his dad was commissioned to seek out ghosts. It's a good way to travel the world, but not a good way to spend as a family.

Rebecca was fine with this castle vacation, but Mavis remembered her saying, "Germany, William? In an old castle chasing ghosts?"

"They are paying well, my dear," he said.

Which was the truth. Mavis didn't know exactly how much, but payment for his dad's services gave them a comfortable life.

So here they were, walking over the moat towards a large drawbridge. To the side, a smaller wooden door eased and creaked open as his dad stepped out.

"Rebecca! Mavis!"

Mavis broke into a sprint and slammed into his dad and gave him a tight hug.

"Mavis! How are you son?"

"I've missed you," Mavis said.

"And I, you. Luckily I haven't been too lonely." William knelt down. "There's been Herman, the castle caretaker. He has one glass eye, so I knew he kept at least one of them on me."

Mavis chuckled.

"William!" Rebecca approached. "That's not nice."

He stood and held the small door open. "Let's go inside. Herman made some hot chocolate and Angel Bread for your arrival."

When they stepped inside, Mavis smelled the hundreds of years of musty odor emanating from the castle's walls. Moss, dirt and water all rolled into one. William noticed Mavis' upturned nose.

"You'll get use to the smell, Mavis," his father said.

"I hope so," Rebecca said, holding her nostrils shut.

The first hallway ran along the side of the castle and disappeared into a corner, turning right. Bulbs hung on sconces on the wall and looked severely out of place with the ancient feel of the castle, but Mavis became thankful for their existence. Something not ancient to remind Mavis of his modern life. Mavis stuck out a hand and drug his finger along the cement wall. The coolness of the stone chilled him and the small little bumps tickled his skin.

"Dad? Have you seen anything yet?" Mavis asked.

"No. But it's still early. One night in a place like this isn't enough. I'm sure I've unsettled someone or something. They're probably mad at me."

They turned the corner and entered a large foyer. The first thing Mavis noticed was a large Oriental rug taking up most of the floor space. It had to be at least thirty feet long and thirty feet wide, if not more. Gold swirls wound and playfully brushed each other on the red background. The middle of the rug sported a sewn square armor insignia. The square was split into four equal colors: starting with the top right quadrant and going clockwise, the patch was red, green, white and green. A small glowing dagger sat where the four squares intersected.

"Is that their coat-of-arms?" Mavis said, standing over the rug.

"Yes. This family's been around for over eight hundred years."

"Really?"

"They are in danger of dying out," William said, "because the last few generations have only produced girls and the two most recent Hvardiscons are without suitors."

"What's a suitor?"

His dad laughed. "Boyfriends."

"Oh."

This got a small chuckle from Rebecca.

His dad continued, "So they believe that whatever haunts this castle is the reason for this hardship and feel if this issue is removed then the daughters will have better luck finding husbands."

"Is this what you believe dad?"

"I just think they're too ugly to find love."

Rebecca stopped them. "William, that's twice!" She turned to Mavis. "Mavis, everyone finds love no matter who they are or what they look like."

"I know Mom. Dad was just joking."

"It's good you know that."

Smiling, William said, "Come on, the dining room's this way."

They passed a set of stone stairs heading into a taller part of the castle Mavis couldn't see. *More darkness.* Though the castle was plain in every which way so far, Mavis knew he would have to explore it to find out what else this place had to offer. His dad can do his work and Mavis could do his.

The old smell of the castle disappeared when Mavis entered the dining room. A subtle chocolate scent drifted into the air and cut out any old damp smell Mavis had just gotten use to. It smelled wonderful.

A door on the other side swung open and a thin, pale man who looked like he could keel over at any moment emerged carrying a silver tray with three cups. Steam curled up and over the edge of the cups and Mavis yearned to taste what created that wonderful smell.

"This is Herman," William introduced. "Herman, this is my wife Rebecca and my son, Mavis."

Herman set the tray on the table and shook Rebecca's hand. "Nice to meet you," he said. He turned to Mavis and held out his hand.

Mavis shook it and stared at Herman's face.

Herman smiled. "I suppose your father told you about my glass eye."

Mavis nodded meekly.

"It's okay, Mavis. It is what it is." Herman raised his finger and tapped his eye. Two *clinks* emitted and Mavis slightly cringed. "It doesn't hurt. The eye is not attached to anything. You want to try?"

"No."

"Suit yourself." Herman pointed to three chairs pulled back from the table. "Have a seat and I will bring out the Angel Bread for you."

They sat down as Herman placed the cups of hot chocolate on the tablemats resting in front of each of them.

"This hot chocolate is from the first hot chocolate store that opened in London in the 1700's," Herman started. "They are still open to this day and produce the beans that make their own powder. Ironically, a Frenchman opened the store and he made millions over the years. Each year, Grandfather Hvardiscon travels to London to buy this chocolate powder in bulk. He buys over two hundred pounds each year. The secret to this hot chocolate is the temperature. It's not over- or under-heated so it won't scald you or tasted thick from being too cold."

Mavis, his mother and father waited until Herman finished the story before lifting the cups to their lips.

The caretaker bowed. "Give me a moment and I will bring the bread." Herman backed himself out of the dining room into the kitchen.

"What do you think of Herman, son?" William asked.

"He's old."

William and Rebecca laughed. A moment later, Herman returned with a platter of Angel Bread. The perfect-looking loaf was extremely fluffy, as if made from the clouds the Angels passed through. He cut three slices and served them on ivory plates. After handing out forks, Herman smiled and said, "If you don't mind, I'm going to head upstairs and do some reading."

"Not at all," William said.

"Excellent. Just leave the dishes on the table. I'll get them later." Herman left the room.

After Herman left, mother, father and son ate the bread and drank the rest of their hot chocolate in silence. Mavis thought the bread was too good to eat and talk at the same time.

When they finished the last crumbs of the bread— and why leave any for fear of missing the taste ever again—they removed themselves from the table and headed upstairs.

3

Mavis's room was twice as large as his room in the States and contained more dressers then he would ever need. His two pieces of luggage sat on the floor near the bed.

The bed loomed over Mavis as he approached it. At first, he wondered if he would be able to get into it, but realized that was a silly thought: he would just climb one of the four thick posts to get on the bed. Then, the plan was to do what every kid did when they spent the night in a bed for the first time. Jump on it.

Mavis lifted his luggage on the bed and unzipped the larger one and removed a small notebook. He flipped through the first pages—which had drawings of trees, fences and houses—until he found a blank page. From a thin pocket in the back of the book Mavis extracted a pencil and took a few steps back. He stared at the bed for a few moments and then began to sketch some lines. The outline soon became the headboard and eventually, Mavis had the entire bed drawn.

He thought about adding the wall, which contained great sweeping patterns of green paisley designs, but boredom set in. Instead, he tossed the pad on the bed and strolled to the window.

The four-paned window was caked with dirt and dust which appeared to be on the inside. Mavis poked his finger into the window and dragged it slowly down to the sill. A clean trail followed the finger. Quickly, he pulled his sleeve over his hand and wiped a fresh circle he could see through.

Mavis had a perfect view of the castle's courtyard, which looked like it hadn't been well taken care of. The yard was wrought with brown, dead patches of grass and weeds twirled up along the outer wall, kidnapping it with a tight grip.

Where were the old cannons and carriages? Mavis thought. *Where were the knights' armor and weapons?*

In the outer wall, Mavis watched a door flap in the wind.

Looking out beyond the wall, Mavis peered at the rolling green hills. Not another house or building in sight. No people tending flocks or taking a stroll.

And it was staring out into the landscape that Mavis drifted off to sleep.

4

Something thudded downstairs.

Mavis jerked away, hitting the top of his head on the window. He rubbed his neck, stretching the kinks out from the awkward position. A muscle relaxed, then snapped loose and he felt better.

Another thud. This one louder.

"Father?" He knew there'd be no answer. His father probably was scouring the castle for the latest assignment.

Mavis stood and went to the door and slowly opened it. Everything sounded normal. Mavis stepped into the hallway and cautiously crept to the top of the stairs.

When he was satisfied there was no other thud coming, he placed his left foot on the next step.

"Aaaaaaagggg!"

His father.

"Dad!"

Instead of an articulate affirmation, a garbled, intense scream slammed Mavis' ears.

"Aaaaaaaggssssh!"

"Dad!"

Mavis sprinted the rest of the way down the stairs and waited a second before realizing that whatever was happening occurred in the foyer of the castle.

He turned towards the foyer and saw a large, blurry flash of white scamper into view.

"Dad!"

"Mavis!" His Mother answered him. "Get out of the castle!"

"Mom!"

"Now!" was his Mother's only reply.

Mavis didn't leave the castle. He made no move towards the doors. Mavis walked into the foyer and what he saw made him grab the door frame. His eyes enlarged and his brain took in too much of the scene and he almost dropped to the floor. Mavis' legs tried to betray him, but grabbing that door frame, as he found out later, was what saved him from suffering the same fate as his Father.

Mavis paused for a moment. It was long enough to hear his mother yell once more before her voice went suddenly silent.

That was enough to send Mavis on his way. He bolted through the entrance and dashed across the bridge and didn't stop running until his legs begged him to stop.

At the crest of a hill, he turned around, saw the top of the castle, then collapsed in the soft grass.

5

When he awoke, Mavis laid on the grass for a moment, forgetting his location. The clouds flowed left to right, hiding the potential of a gorgeous night sky. The breeze pushed the clouds, caressing Mavis' face.

"Mother!"

Mavis sat up looking around. Hills and grass and deep dusk.

He ran as fast as he could back to the castle. His chest pressed into his body when he finally reached the bridge. Mavis stopped in the middle of the bridge. He checked out the wall in front of him, then moved his eyes from window to window. When Mavis felt sure he was safe, he cautiously crept across the bridge to the door he and his mother had met his father just hours ago.

He stepped through, eyes closed the entire time.

Once he reached what he thought was the foyer, Mavis slowly opened his eyelids. Before him, he remembered why he ran from the castle.

Mavis leaned his head to see a little more of what remained in the main entrance hall.

Blood dots lined the wall as if a waterfall of blood ran down the stones. Some blood was in smeared streaks while most of it managed to decorate the wall in a morbid connect-the-dots puzzle Mavis use to do in his early years of school.

He didn't want to enter the hall, but he knew he had to know. Mavis had to see.

Mavis took quiet, simple steps as he frantically shifted his head around. Too much invaded his eyes. Too much disaster in one area. He saw furniture turned over and snapped into pieces, rugs ripped to shreds, and long, deep scratches across the walls.

His father draped over the banister of the stairs. His back arched in a way that seemed impossible, like he had no spine. *Limber as a snake*, Mavis thought. Other limbs of his father's sprouted in ridiculous directions, dripping blood below. A large, circular puddle formed from William's head and as Mavis got closer, he saw a huge string of blood emerge from the gash in his father's chest.

"Father," Mavis whispered.

Mavis raised his hands to close his father's eyes. "I'm sorry I couldn't save you," he said. He used his palm to shut the eyelids. As he did so, he saw his mother's legs protruding from a doorway.

Blurry trails of blood extended from her feet. *She probably died in here and was dragged into there*, he thought. Mavis wondered if she suffered or died immediately.

A hot liquid rose in his stomach, climbing into his throat. It burned, forcing an escape. His jaws spasmed—

Mavis turned and sprinted back outside, puking all over the ground. The second, harder lurch brought up small clots of blood. He wiped his mouth, then crossed the bridge. He couldn't go back in there. He couldn't imagine looking at that scene one more time, his father and mother dying so violently.

6

"And I didn't go back in there," Mavis said to me. "I never saw my mother's face again. If I knew it had all been like that, I would have passed on seeing my father, but I didn't know."

"How could you know?" I said.

Mavis nodded. "Yes, I suppose so."

The tale Mavis spewed for me lasted about an hour, but with the table full of empty beer cans in front of us, I thought for certain it was the morning.

"And what after that?" I asked.

"I've been tracking ghosts ever since then." Mavis finished the beer he held then stretched his back. "My goodness, I didn't think that story would last so long."

"Ghosthunter Jones," I murmured. "Is that why you're obsessed with banshees?"

"What? Obsessed?"

"Yes, for killing your mother and father."

Mavis thought for a second. "I guess so. I never really thought about it, but I have always hoped to encounter a banshee. Never have, until now. The crazy thing is that your call is the first call that I've ever had for a banshee."

"Really? That inspires confidence."

"Don't get asinine on me. I know you had nothing to do with those murders or deaths or whatever you want to call them. Mr. Hamilton and others might think you did, but if they knew what I knew and experienced what I have, then those non-believers would know the truth."

I laughed.

"What's so funny?" Mavis asked.

"'Non-believers? You sound like a crazy religious fanatic." I paused. "What truth do you know?"

He shrugged. "That you didn't do it."

"It would help if we had proof."

"I know. I know," he said. "We'll sort this out, Grant, we will."

"I hope so. I can't live in this town too much longer if everyone thinks I'm a murderer."

"Don't give up," he said. "Innocence is best remembered and respect is magnified when accusations fly and are false."

"That's interesting. Who said that?"

"My father. People always thought he did bad things everywhere he went to investigate the paranormal. When things were said and done and when he proved himself, respect for him increased phenomenally."

I saw his eyes well up with tears, but the old ghosthunting softie held them back.

7

Mavis and I watched some TV to relax the rest of the night. He eventually fell asleep on the couch. I woke up about 3 a.m. and went to my own bed. I didn't go back to sleep. Instead, I wondered how Mavis was going to help me with the banshee and help me figure out this whole shitstorm.

The old ghosthunter was actually fun and interesting to have around, but the fact of the matter remained: people suspected me of murder.

CHAPTER TWELVE

1

A ringing phone jolted me awake.

My clock flashed 12:00, so whatever time it was, my body felt exhausted. I remember being up at 3 a.m., but that's it. I flipped my legs over the edge of the bed and sat there for a minute rubbing my eyes.

"Grant!" I heard from the other room.

What the hell—

"Grant! Phone!" It was Mavis. Then last night flooded back into my mind: his parents; his quest for the Banshee; my feeling of going to jail and receiving the death penalty for all my crimes.

I chuckled. Someone's crimes. The banshee's crimes. How did you arrest a ghost? Bobby might know how since he's the best cop this town has seen.

I laughed. *The best this town has seen. Good one, Grant.*

"Grant, get your ass down here and take this call!"

I stood and went downstairs.

Mavis held the phone to me when I entered the room. In his other hand, a beer.

"Isn't it a little early for that?" I said, pointing to the beer.

"It's 2 p.m."

I leaned back and caught a glimpse of the clock on the oven. Damn, 2 p.m. indeed.

"Shit," I said. "Who is it?"

"Maggie."

I shook my head. I mouthed the word 'NO' and starting backing away.

Mavis rose and came towards me with the phone. It's moments like this I wished the phone was corded so I could escape into the bathroom. Mavis would only get so far.

Instead, he caught up to me and pressed the phone into my chest.

"You'll want to take this," he whispered.

2

"Hello," I said into the phone.

"Hi Grant." Maggie. Her voice sounded calm, trusting.

"What can I do for you?"

"You ask that like I'm buying a car from you."

"Well?" *She* called *me*, what did she expect?

"Listen," she said. "I want to tell you something. I don't have much time." She paused for a moment. "Grant, I must tell you that I know you didn't kill anyone. The town is just rampant with rumor and while there's quite a bit of evidence pointing in your direction, I don't believe you killed anyone."

"I appreciate that, Maggie, I do, but I must be honest with you and say I don't hear it in your voice."

Another pause. *What the fuck was going on over there?*

"I can't speak too loud. You'll have to trust me. Can we meet somewhere? Maybe at Triumph Park for a walk?"

She knew how to get me. Triumph Park was the first park we ever took a walk in and the park where I told her I thought things could happen where we'd be more than friends. It turned out that friends were all anything we'd be.

"I guess. When?"

I heard scuffling on the other end. "How about an hour?" She offered.

"*Maggie, come in here!*" That was also on Maggie's end.

"What was that?" I asked. More importantly, *who* was that?

"Nothing. An hour then?"

"*Maggie, come in the bedroom. Something's come up!*" Then idiotic laughter. Oddly, I swore that was Bobby's voice.

"Is that the Chief making some ridiculous innuendo about his dick?"

Maggie sighed. "One hour. Triumph Park."

"Fine."

She hung up.

"So..." Mavis said. "Was it a good idea to take it or not?"

"At first. Then it made me sick."

He tilted his head like confused dog and I shooed the look away. "I'm going to Triumph Park in an hour," I said.

"Romantic."

"I'm sure it has nothing to do with romance."

"I hope things work out at the park. I think I'll hit up that forest again, then maybe sneak to Betty's house again. Take some more readings."

"Mavis." I stopped myself. I didn't really know what I wanted to ask. I think I wanted him to reassure me that he would find something. That he would have the answer to all my problems. But I didn't ask anything. I didn't want him to tell me everything was going to be all right, when it appeared that nothing was going to be all right. Sure it's what I wanted to hear, but a deep, horrible feeling inside my bowels told me it wouldn't be the truth.

"What?" Mavis walked to me and took a long look into my eyes. He saw something there and I'm positive I sent out the look of despair, but he let it go. "Never mind, I suppose. See you later?"

"How about more of that talk and beer time?" I struggled to for a smile.

Mavis nodded. "Sure thing. Whenever you get home or vice versa."

He palmed my shoulder and gave it a little squeeze. Just like my father did. Without another word, he left.

3

One hour seemed like five when counting on another person to show, so I didn't rush and grabbed myself a beer.

May as well get an early start.

As I tilted back the first swallow of the beer, a crash filtered down into the living room.

"Mavis?" No, he had already left.

I stood, setting my beer in the fridge on my way to the stairs. The beer would settle, but hopefully I could get back to it in a few minutes.

The stairs elongated before my eyes and I looked up and saw the banshee. Her blurry aura mocked me at the top of the stairs. The tendrils of dress reached out to me like snakes coming for the kill. Luckily, I was too far away.

She turned and floated out of sight.

Dammit. Of course I'd have to follow. What kind of chance did I or Mavis have if I couldn't see her intentions?

Mavis! I reached inside of my pocket for my cell phone, but remembered it sat on the side table in the living room. No time to get it.

I trotted up the stairs and stopped at the landing. I turned my head down the hall and saw the trails of her dress disappearing into my bedroom.

Why is she going in there? What is that bitch up to?

Sticking to the wall across my bedroom, I scooted along until I began to see the furniture. First, a desk came into view, then the desk chair, then an old rocker my grandmother gave me. Whatever possessed her to give me an old oak rocker was a testament to how crazy she was. Never had I used a rocker and never would I need a rocker. My grandmother use to be that crazy old bat that lived at the end of the block that everyone made fun of.

My bed was against the wall adjacent to the hallway. The end of the bed became visible and I had to actually take a step away from my wall in order to see more bed.

I saw part of the woman hovering over my bed.

I eased myself to the door jamb and crept into my room. She faced the window, gazing into the darkness. I stood in front of my desk, reaching back for a weapon, anything I could use for protection or attack. I was sure anything I'd use would harm the banshee, but I'd have to try.

A deep, grinding sound echoed in the bedroom and second later, the woman slowly turned in my direction. The sound deepened and then creaked to a stop, with the woman now staring intently at me. Was she on some kind of platform? What the hell made that sound?

Then, she inched her way toward me, her eyes boring their way into my own. Her mouth opened and closed, like she meant to say something, then thought better of it because she would offend me.

Or she prepared to eat my flesh.

She passed the bed and only floated three feet from me. I glanced at the door and this movement must have also been in her head because as I leapt towards the door, it slammed shut.

I hit the door hard, stunned. I stayed upright for only a moment, then my legs gave out and my body collapsed to the floor.

My head swam, a million clouds forming in front of my eyes. As my eyes fluttered, I saw the banshee ease close to me. But that was all I'd see at this second—

4

When I turned eighteen, my grandmother threw a huge party for me. "It's your induction into life," she told me. "It's the moment that you become a man."

Perfect, Grandma, what if I didn't want to become a man?

Grandma Sykes was very religious. Many things in her life revolved around Church, God and Jesus. Prayers at every meal; Church on Sunday mornings and Wednesday evenings; and multiple Church groups throughout the week. Before my mother and father died, each time we'd visit Grandma, I was assured a very intense visit with Grandma and God. I think because her son stopped going to Church when he moved out, she figured him a lost cause. And my mom? Grandma never like her anyway.

So Grandma Sykes took it upon herself to make sure that I didn't forget about God and Jesus and how he is my savior. The first thing she would say to me wasn't "Hello," but "Grant, do you accept Jesus as your Lord and Savior?" My answer was always yes, whether I thought He was my Lord and Savior or not. It would break her heart if I said no.

On my eighteenth birthday, Grandma, my two best friends John and Kari and I attended my party. Both of them had decided to take the same journalism career path as me so we all just kind of bonded our senior year. Grandma asked if I wanted to invite anyone else, but I just wanted to keep it simple.

For the afternoon, the three of us sat in the living room chatting about the future, our summer plans and things we enjoyed the most from our past year. Grandma pretty much stayed in the kitchen: first making us lunch, and then finishing the cake.

After celebrating my birthday and the final months of senior year, John and Kari left. We made plans to head out to Victory's for a night of bowling around 7. I wanted to relax for the rest of the afternoon after they left, but when I heard my grandmother's scream, I knew it would not happen. I didn't relax for days.

I ran to the kitchen and didn't see her.

Something flew by the window. Floating dark hair speckled with white. I knew that was my grandmother and I dashed through the back door.

To my left, my 87-year-old grandmother sat against the side of the house.

"Grandma!" I yelled. I jumped the five steps off the porch and pounded each foot into the ground as I made my way to her. When I was a few feet away I heard,

"No, Grant. Stay away." Her voice was hardly there. Less than a whisper.

I knelt down. "What?"

"Stay away. Leave." A little more forceful this time, but still nearly non-existent.

"Let me help you."

She shook her head.

Then I saw her eyes focus on something behind me.

I turned and saw her. The banshee. The bitch who murdered my mother and father in the woods.

"What's going on Grandma?"

"You need to get out of here."

"No. Grab my arm."

"She won't let you help me."

"Who is she?"

"You know." She let her tired eyes fixate on my face. "It is my time. Just like when it was your mother's time and your father's time."

"No," I said, but the quiver in my voice didn't reassure me.

"You know this."

Except I didn't know. I just knew that my family was disappearing because of her.

"Go Grant. I won't ask you again."

I backed away. Something in her eyes pushed me back; I realized it was what must be done.

As I continued to move backwards, the banshee closed the space between it and my grandmother. The further I got, the closer the woman got. My grandmother remained still as the white, jabbing gown of the banshee reached for the frail old woman. Grandma lifted her face to the woman and closed her yes.

The banshee slightly lowered herself and then two paper-thin arms extended—

I turned completely around and sprinted to the opposite of the house. I couldn't watch. I knew the outcome and I did not want to see.

I plastered myself against the wall and slid down until my butt rested on the ground. In my mind, I sensed I mirrored the same position as my Grandmother, only on this side.

Seconds later, I felt a small vibration ride my spine.

Was that it? No noise? No scream?

I stuttered awake and it took me a few minutes to realize I was lying on the floor in my own bedroom. Sweat soaked the carpet where my head rested and I felt quick jabs of pain circling around the crown of my head. I attempted to sit up, but I had to close my eyes in order to stop the nausea that rose in my stomach.

When I saw the banshee, everything came back: the noise, my stupidity in checking it out, getting knocked to the floor. And watching my grandmother die again.

I sobbed for a moment, staring at the woman.

The air around her pulsated as she brought up her hands and crept towards me.

This is it, I thought. Now, killing the entire family will be complete for her.

She went over the edge of the bed and instead of continuing to float at the same height, she dropped down to my level. There was no stopping. Her body easily penetrated through the floor all the way to her neck. Before she completely disappeared, the banshee turned her head to me. Since she paused about a foot from me, the scream she belted threw a thousand sharp points into my ears.

"Fuuuuuuuck!" I yelled, backing into the hall.

I ran downstairs to the living room, which was located under my bedroom, just in time to see the bottom half of the banshee vanish through the outer wall.

The alarm on my watch chimed.

Maggie. Park. I almost forgot.

A light mist fell as I pulled into the park and shut off the engine. Dusk slowly crept around me. Ahead, Maggie sat on a bench, scrunching her body against the chill. The sprinkle must have surprised her: no umbrella. If there was one person prepared before I or anyone else knew to be prepared, it was Maggie.

My plain blue umbrella rested in the back seat. Purchased by Maggie for me. Used twice, both times for Maggie's benefit when we got caught in the rain together.

When we were together.

Two years? Three? I couldn't remember. I pushed my brain back to the time immediately after I came back to Ilton. I couldn't place the moments Maggie and I spent together. I only recalled one or two moments. That seemed unfair to spend such a long time together and to just have it disappear over time. I wondered if the same occurred with her. Memories are crazy that way, I suppose.

When I got out and shut the door, Maggie lifted her head and waved. I nodded and popped open the umbrella and walked to her.

A smile I had not seen in quite a long time formed on her face.

"You're here," she said.

"Yes, I said I would be." I sat down and shifted some of the umbrella to cover her.

"Thanks for that," she said, pointing to the umbrella.

I nodded. "What's so pressing that you left the Chief to come here?"

The smile faded slightly. "Shush. This is more than just that."

"Okay, then just what is it?"

Maggie twisted her body towards mine. I remembered she use to do this when she was about to say some serious things. She took her hands out of her pockets and used them both to grab my free hand. This was going to be very, *very* serious.

Wait a minute. This was how she positioned herself when she let me go years ago. When she broke my heart. "This is what you did when you broke up with me," I said. "Do you remember?"

She nodded once. "I do. But that was then. I want to tell you something now."

"So tell me."

"First, I'm sorry I didn't believe you. Let me just say that first."

"About what?"

"You know: about the murders. I was wrong to suspect you had even an inkling of knowledge or direct action in those deaths." As an after-thought, she added, "Mr. Noonan obviously collapsed from a heart attack."

"Obviously," I said.

"And the others, well, that's just too strange. To me, it seems you want these problems fixed just like the rest of the town. Is Mr. Jones the fix?"

"Hopefully, but what is the big deal now? So you don't think I killed those people. The rest of the town does, especially your Chief Bobby Hamilton. Maggie, I appreciate the sentiment, but there's nothing you can do or say that will make this go away. Mavis and I are working on it." I lifted my hand from hers. "Sure, we don't know what's going on right now, but he's good. He knows what he's doing."

"I'm sure he does, Grant. Do you?"

She asked, but I didn't know my competence in the matter. Not ghosts, just my sanity. "Do I give the impression that I don't?" I asked.

She shrugged. "I don't know. You seem haunted by something."

There it was. The word 'haunted.' Yes, I am haunted, Maggie, thanks for asking. The banshee was probably right around the corner, ready to pounce if you crossed her. Then that would make what? Five people close to me that had died at the screams of that *bitch*? Would Maggie really count? She's not part of my family.

I glanced around just to make sure we weren't being stalked.

"I wouldn't say haunted. My mind's just weighed down from it all."

Maggie squinted, trying to find something deeper within my last statement, something deeper in my voice to indicate I was fibbing a little. If she stared long enough, I'm sure she'd find it.

"*That's all*," I emphasized.

"That's all?"

I nodded.

"How did you get to this point? The point where you had to call a ghosthunter to help you?" She asked.

"I just reached that point, I guess."

"And what about this point for us?"

"What do you mean?" Really, where was she going with this? "This point for us? Where is there an *us* except for work? "

"The point where you resent me for dating Bobby," she said.

"You created that path when you broke up with me and began holding Bobby's stick in your hands."

"Grant, be serious. You can't resent me that much."

"Yes, no. Maybe. I'm not sure. Things changed, that's one thing I'm sure happened." I looked away and watched a stray Black Labrador root around a large lilac bush. The lilacs would soon deplete, giving in to the coming fall. The dog smelled something good, pawed at the ground and moved on.

"You made them change," Maggie said.

"Did I? I don't recall facilitating the break-up."

"Emotionally, you did."

I shook my head. "There's a difference between losing touch and wanting to get things rolling. It all took me by surprise." I handed her the umbrella. "Keep this if you're staying out here."

"Where are you going?"

"Home. Sleep, eat, drink. I don't know. Anything but listening to this and talking about our past."

"Our past is us."

"Us! *Us* is a professional relationship. That's the only relationship I can tolerate with you. Seeing you outside of work rips my heart in two every single fucking time!"

Maggie leaned back, a little shock on her face.

"I still have feelings for you!" I finished.

I stood and took a few steps away.

A hand grabbed my arm and stopped me. I turned and saw Maggie standing inches from me.

"I know," she whispered. "I know."

"What?"

She didn't say anything else. Maggie leaned in and raised her mouth to mine.

Her warm lips sent lightning bolts of pleasure through my body. Maggie's tongue separated my own lips and intertwined with my tongue. Our breathing quickened and my hands cupped her face and pushed her head further into mine as I tried to get closer and more into her.

As we kissed, the rest of her body pressed against mine and my cock hardened in a matter of seconds. She must have felt this because she jammed her body into it and shifted into my hard-on with her body.

Was this what I wanted? A quick sexual rendezvous in the park after all these years?

Maggie's hands lowered and grasped my cock through my jeans. She squeezed. My breath burst into her mouth and she broke free and moaned.

"Yes, Grant," she murmured.

She took one of her hands, grabbed one of mine and placed it on her breast. I couldn't really feel anything through her coat, but I rubbed the left breast anyway. She gasped and clinched my cock harder.

"No," I said.

I removed my hand from her breast and shoved her hand from my cock that pushed uncomfortably on my jeans. I took one step back, just far enough to distance myself from the passion that was about to get more heated.

"What-what do you mean no?" Maggie stammered.

"I can't do this."

"Grant, don't you understand what I'm doing?"

"No, I don't," I answered. "Do you just want to get laid?"

"What the fuck are you saying?"

"You heard me: do you just want to get laid? Is Bobby not doing it for you?"

Her hand flew across my cheek. My head jerked to the side and the sting of the slap intensified for a moment before slowly fading away. I rubbed my cheek to deaden the pain and to deaden my pride.

"You know what? I shouldn't have come out here to throw myself at you. Do you realize I still have feelings for you too?"

"Why haven't you said anything before? Three years? Each of us going through relationships as the other feels this way? Why didn't you say anything?" I took another step back just in case Maggie wanted to let loose with another slap. She didn't, and I was glad, she hit pretty well.

"How could I have said anything with fear that we would just jump back into it starting off the same as when we left it? No improvement, no difference, no change."

"But if I had known…"

"You can say that now," she said, "because it's out on the table now and there's no chance of anything happening tonight or ever."

I stood there, waiting for more biting words from Maggie's mouth, but apparently she was done. She sat back down on the bench, still holding my blue umbrella. She could keep that.

"Good night," I said.

"Sure."

The walk back to my car was desolate. I felt the trip completely lonely: no Maggie behind me, no stray dog to distract me, and for a second, I thought I saw my car disappear. My stomach dropped. My eyes scanned the ground as I walked and I nearly ran into my car, but I looked up at the last second and paused before opening the door.

I started the car and watched Maggie throw one quick glance towards me before she stood and left. As I backed away, I watched the stray dog from earlier reappear and approach the bench I just came from. He sniffed around, hopped up on the bench and smelled the spots where Maggie and I had just sat. He found nothing. I put the car in drive and the Lab, slightly frightened, whipped his head in my direction. He leapt from the bench and sprinted through the lilac bushes.

I know how you feel buddy. I know how you feel.

6

Mavis slumbered on the couch, a bottle of beer hanging precariously from his fingertips. Light snores escaped his mouth and I caught his eyes darting back and forth under the eyelids. A dream. Hopefully a wonderful dream.

I slipped the bottle from his hand and set it on the coffee table, then turned off all the lights and headed upstairs.

In my room, I shut the door, then closed all the drapes. I flipped the light switch and I stood in my room in total darkness.

I lied down without pulling back the covers and just let my body wind down for the night. It didn't take long for me to fall asleep.

—how long was I asleep before I saw myself standing in a desert. Not a complete desert: I could see a patch of green in the distance. A patch of grassy land, I presumed.

To my left was more sand and an extension of the grass. To my right and behind me, the same: a section of desert surrounded by grass.

Why was I here?

As if someone or something heard my question, sand began swirling about fifteen feet ahead of me. It rose higher until it reminded me of the dust devils that I use to chase in Ilton during the hot, dry summers when I was younger.

The first sand tornado matched my height another started to form next to it, then another, then another and another. A total of seven spinning sand cones appeared before me.

And slowly each one started to take shape.

First, my father. Then, my mother. Grandmother, Betty, Mr. Noonan, Pete, and finally Miss Molly.

Everyone that had died at the hands of the banshee stood before me as Sand People.

They stared. Stared with an intensity that sent tingles through my stomach and brain. But when I turned, piles of sand washed over my feet and held me in place.

From the left, I heard a hollow wind rise up. It came close rather quickly and stirred some sand up next to Miss Molly.

The new Sand Person was Maggie.

"Maggie!" I yelled.

Another violent wind rustled another additional Sand Person.

Me.

I saw each feature formed exactly as I stood in this sand now.

My Sand Clone was the first to disappear and then as quickly as they appeared, the Sand People vanished back into the sand.

And everything was quiet again.

—It couldn't have been more than an hour, but when I turned on my side, the clock read 3:42. A.M. Fuck, it's been six hours and it's now in the fresh of the morning. Stay up or lay back down? I could get another three hours sleep and start the day ready to vanquish the banshee. Would nine hours of sleep be enough? Or too much? How much of the sleeping reports was true. If you were trying to defend yourself against a ghost that was taking the lives of people around you then you needed as much sleep as you could get.

Yeah, that's what I'll do.

Laying back down wins the race.

CHAPTER THIRTEEN

1

A heavy pounding bounded through the house as I opened my eyes. What was that?

It took about ten more slams before I realized that someone was at the door. Then it took five seconds to physically get out of bed because I wondered why Mavis hadn't answered the door yet. He had practically moved in, why couldn't he get the door?

I sprinted downstairs and saw Mavis scrambling from the couch as I went by.

"What?" he said, still groggy. "What is that noise?"

"The door," I said. "It's the door."

I almost ran into the door as I opened it. Bobby stood there, with a stern face.

"Bobby," I said.

Behind him, his police car sat half on the street, half on the sidewalk. The thin red and blue lights device spun around and around in that hypnotizing way that made you stop to look at accidents or nearly shit your pants when the cops pulled you over.

"What's up?" I asked.

"You are under arrest, Grant Sykes."

"Arrest?"

"Grant, what's going on?" Mavis asked behind me.

"Apparently, I'm under arrest," I said.

Turning back to Bobby, I said, "Under arrest for what?"

"The murder and rape of Maggie Johnson," he said.

"You're kidding, right. I'm seriously under arrest?" I looked back at Mavis, who shrugged.

"Yes. I'm asking this not as a question, but as more advice: are you coming peacefully?"

"What proof do you have?" I asked.

"Enough." He stepped inside the door and removed his handcuffs from the case. "Turn around."

"Mavis?" What was I suppose to do? Go or not go were my two options.

Mavis shrugged again. "Go with him. I'll see what I can do about bond and figuring out what's going on."

"No bond, sir," Bobby said. "No bond will be set for days."

"Won't he be arraigned tomorrow morning?" Mavis asked. "Today is Wednesday, so there's no reason he can't get in front of a judge tomorrow."

"We'll see."

Chief fucking Bobby Hamilton turned me around and I felt the cold steel of the handcuffs trap my wrists. Four clicks each side.

"Do they have to be so tight?" I asked him. They dug into my skin and each movement rubbed deeper.

"For murderers they do."

"Do you have to be a complete dick?"

"Are you badgering a police officer?"

Mavis coughed. "Grant. Settle down. Go quietly. We'll figure this out."

"I doubt it," Bobby said.

Bobby led me from my house and down the sidewalk to his car. My neighbors found the combination of the lighted squad car and Bobby guiding me from my house interesting: a small group of about fifteen formed in the street.

"Move away from the police car," he said. "Make room!"

Slowly, the group dispersed, but still congregated in three or four person clusters. I felt everyone's eyes on me and I sense their thoughts. *What did he do? Where is he going? Why is he handcuffed? Who will bail him out? When will he go to court for whatever he's going in for? Who could I talk to that might know? What gossip can I make up about this?* The questions began with the basic fundamental questions used in journalism: who, what, where, when and why. How was a question I needed to find out for myself because whatever Bobby had on me was false. How he got whatever he had on me was a mistake.

Bobby opened the back door and pushed me into the back seat. "Thank you driver," I said.

"Shut the fuck up, Grant," he whispered.

He slammed the door, then plopped into the driver's seat. He picked up his radio handset.

"Gina, car one coming in," he said.

Through static, "Um, okay, Chief."

When Bobby backed the car off the sidewalk and began moving forward, I leaned into the grating separating me from Bobby.

"Do you really believe I raped and murdered Maggie?" I asked him. "How can you possibly think that?"

He shrugged.

"What proof do you have?" I asked.

"As I said before, enough."

"I don't think you have any."

"If that's what you think, then so be it." He accelerated slightly. "No more talking. It will all be sorted out at the station."

I crashed back into the seat, defeated.

I suppose I'll have to wait and see how much will be sorted out. Hopefully, Mavis will figure something out.

2

Bobby pulled into one of the three open parking spots in front of the community hall. He exited the car, then opened my door. I eased my out legs and when I angled my head out, Bobby grabbed the collar of my shirt and assisted me by tugging me from the car the rest of the way.

"Thanks a lot," I said sarcastically, which I knew wasn't going to get me nowhere with a prick like Bobby.

"Move," he commanded.

It was just me and Bobby

—me and bobby hamilton mcgee—

out here in front of the community hall. I wondered if I could outrun Bobby in a footrace. Lazy-ass would probably jump in his car to chase me. I really wouldn't have a chance because there would be no place I could really go. I was already banished by everyone in town. And with Ilton seven miles from any other town, I would be caught again and in more trouble than ever. Mavis would have no chance for any type of defense.

My body wanted to run, but my mind knew better. I continued walking towards the community hall doors.

When I reached the doors, I paused to let Bobby open them. "It's nice being catered to," I said.

He ignored me this time and waited for me to go by.

Inside, Gina stood when I entered. "Hey, Grant," she said. "Is it—"

Bobby interrupted her. "Gina, go unlock the cell and prepare it for the prisoner."

She went to the back of the room, and unlocked the only door in the hall.

Bobby pulled a chair to his desk. "Sit," he said. "We need to talk."

"If you are so sure I'm the suspect, then I'd like a lawyer."

"That is your right."

"You better believe that's my fucking right."

"I suppose you want to make your phone call now then."

I smiled. "Another one of my fucking rights."

Bobby latched onto the phone at his desk and set it down in front of me. He leaned back in his chair as I picked up the receiver.

"Privacy, please?" I said.

He shook his head.

"Noted," I said. "The proper people will be informed." Even thought I smiled, my plan of unnerving him had no effect.

"So," is all he said.

I dialed Mavis' number and he quickly answered. "Hey there," he said. "I figured I'd receive your phone call."

"Yeah, well, it's a little strange down here," I said. "What's up?"

"Can you come down here so we can talk?"

"Am I allowed?"

"Sure why not? You know what to do," I paused, "to get down here right?"

Mavis kept silent on his end. "I think so," he finally said. "I should pretend to be a lawyer, correct?"

I laughed. "You got it now!"

I slammed the phone down. "He's on his way."

"Who is your lawyer?" Bobby asked.

"I answer no questions until he gets here."

"Fine." He stood and jangled the handcuff keys. "Stand and turn around."

Gina appeared from the cell and threw down the extra blankets and toiletries she removed from the cell. "Chief, it's ready," she said.

"In the cell until your lawyer gets here," Bobby said.

I entered the cell and didn't turn around to see the door close and the lock click.

They called it a cell, but it was more of just a simple room. The ten by ten area held a cot, a toilet, a sink, and a small fold-out table meant to be a desk. The walls were white and the floor made from tile. A medium-sized fluorescent light encased in plastic cascaded down a dull yellow. The only window was on the door leading to the main room, and it was just big enough to put my face through and see what went on the other side. On a positive note, the bright room could possibly alleviate any depression anyone might have if forced to stay in here for an extended period of time.

On the negative side, I was being accused of raping and murdering the one person I had ever loved.

I lied down on the cot and waited for Mavis.

3

The community hall walls shuttered when the main doors opened. I jumped up and looked through the door window to see Mavis enter. Surprisingly, I could not hear the conversation between Mavis and Bobby.

Mavis had switched from his "ghosthunting" clothes to something more presentable: slacks, dress shirt and a blazer. He spoke some words to Bobby, who shook his head in response to what was said. Mavis said something else, then Bobby looked to the side— presumably to Gina—then indicated to my cell.

A few seconds later, I heard a key slide into the lock and then a few clicks. I stepped back as the door opened outward and Gina said, "Mr. Jones is here for you Grant."

"Thanks, Gina," I said.

Mavis nodded to Gina as he walked past and closed the door behind him. He surveyed my cell and smiled. "Nice digs here," he said.

"It's cozy. You have some nice threads."

"They're cozy."

A little chuckle escaped my mouth. "How did you get Bobby to let you in here?"

"I'm your lawyer."

"Well, I knew that, but what about Bobby?"

Mavis handed me a paper. "This is my license to practice in the State of Illinois."

Glancing at the paper, I saw that it looked pretty damn official. A State of Illinois seal, a signature of the Attorney General that looked genuine and all on thick parchment paper that no one in a small town would contest.

"I borrowed your computer," he said. "I hope you don't mind."

"Of course not. It's good to have a Ghosthunter who's also a lawyer."

"Yeah." He leaned in. "So did he tell you anything?" Mavis' voice lowered.

"You don't have to talk lower. I can't hear anything out there so I assume they can't hear anything out there. Besides, Gina doesn't care." I shook my head. "But no, Bobby didn't say anything about anything."

"You and I know something's strange about this."

"We can't prove anything."

"Not here, we can't," Mavis said.

"We? I won't see a judge until tomorrow—if he lets me even then—and by that time, who knows what kind of lies Bobby will spread."

"Yes," Mavis agreed, "tomorrow will be too late. That's why I will be back later tonight to remedy *that* situation."

The look on my face, I'm sure, seemed questioning. "And how will that happen?"

He waved his hand around the room. "Look at this place. No bars, no complicated locks, no guards. This place is just inviting me to bust you out."

"I guess, but don't you think we should take our chances with the courts? I can probably get bail."

"How confident are you in that? I don't think you will, especially if Bobby has anything to say about it." Mavis stood up. "Be ready to leave at midnight."

"A midnight break out. Just like in the movies."

Mavis laughed. "No better time."

"Okay. Then what?"

"What do you think? Is there anyone that could help us?"

I thought for a moment. "No, not off the top of my head. I think we should assume no one will help us."

"That's fine," Mavis said. "I think when we figure out who killed Maggie, we will find out who set you up."

I nodded.

"See you tonight," Mavis said.

He knocked on the door and Gina appeared. Close behind, Bobby stood with his hand on his gun.

"Seriously, Bobby?" I yelled out.

He knew what I meant because he answered, "For a rapist? Yes."

4

I continually checked the desk clock sitting on Gina's desk to keep track of the time. I was fed lunch—a nice burger meal from *Betty's*—a small afternoon snack (an apple and block of cheese leftover from Bobby's lunch, courtesy of Gina, I'm sure,) and before Bobby and Gina left for the night, dinner at 5:30. Dinner consisted of meatloaf, potatoes, and a pile of corn, all from *Betty's*. At least I had my favorite food from my favorite restaurant.

Gina opened the door and handed me the Styrofoam container with the food and a can of Pepsi. "Sleep well," she said.

I said thanks and hope you have a good night and she asked if I needed anything else. Before I could answer, Bobby called her away, berating her for "commiserating with a prisoner." She shut the door and I heard her laugh, telling Bobby I was no prisoner, just the subject of a cruel joke. I popped my head in the window and they continued to talk, but I couldn't hear them.

5:45.

At 6:30, I lied down. It would still be another five hours and thirty minutes until Mavis sprung me, so a little nap was definitely in order.

5

When I woke, I wondered how long I'd been asleep. I rose with a jolt and dove for the door. A tiny emergency light illuminated the outer office just enough for me to see that it was 11:40. Just in time. I would have been kicking myself if I wasn't awake when Mavis arrived. I didn't know what Mavis had in mind to free me, but I'm sure he couldn't have me slumbering.

I nibbled on the last of my meatloaf. One thing about Betty's meatloaf recipe was that it was good hot from the oven or good at room temperature. I dipped a chunk of the meat in the small swirl of potatoes. Unfortunately, I didn't have the same sentiment for the potatoes as I had for the meatloaf.

With my little snack digesting, I cupped some water from the sink in my hand and slurped. I shut the water off and then heard a muffled crash.

At the window, I scanned the room for any breach. All the windows were intact.

The main doors jiggled and finally, the right door eased open. A beam of light crept through the door and flipped over to one side of the room. The door widened and a leg came through. Then, a body.

Mavis walked in, jerking the beam of a flashlight across the room. The light swung to the window, blinding me for moment. He came over and I saw him lift something high and then arc it towards the ground.

A *clink* came and the door opened.

"Hello there, prisoner!" Mavis shone the light on my face and I squinted.

"Hey there. Appreciate a little less light in the face."

Mavis removed the light.

"What's in your hands?" I asked.

He lifted two doorknobs up into light. Both silver knobs were from the community hall. One from the front door and one from my cell door. "Subtle," I commented.

"Let's go," Mavis said. "I know the whole town is sleeping—"

"But you probably woke the town with that banging of yours."

Mavis turned. "It had to be done."

On the way out, I grabbed the envelope with my stuff and followed Mavis out the door. His car sat next to Bobby's police car and I hopped in the passenger side.

Mavis got in, started the car and we pulled out. His eyes stared intently ahead.

"Got a destination in mind?" I asked.

"I do," he answered. "And I don't think you're going to like it one bit."

"Where?"

"Where Maggie was killed."

6

Maggie lived on the outskirts of town, in a small white, ranch house with a huge front yard. I recalled mowing that beast of a yard at least once a week years ago when Maggie and I were together. After a rain, the grass needed mowing; after a humid spell, the grass needed mowing; after you looked at it, the yard needed mowing. She had minimal landscaping that needed done, so I got lucky in that regards. At the moment, the grass was longer than I ever allowed or would have let it. Bobby wasn't keeping up on his boyfriendly duties.

Mavis pulled into the driveway and shut off the lights and rolled another twenty feet before stopping. The car clock read just a little after midnight.

"Did she live alone?" Mavis asked.

"Unless Bobby stayed over, yes."

"I doubt he's here tonight," he said.

We both got out of the car, making sure to lightly close our doors. I stood in the driveway, realizing it had been years since I had been inside Maggie's house. Unfortunately, the circumstances that required me to finally enter the house were not those I had ever hoped for.

"Back door," he whispered.

Mavis unlocked the wooden gate and waited for me to pass before shutting it. We crept along the side of the house until we hit the back yard. I noticed an above ground pool, about four feet tall and about sixteen feet wide. She must have gotten this after we broke up. She always complained about the summer heat. Whether it was dry or humid, the heat was always unbearable to Maggie.

As we passed the pool, I drug my hand across the water. I imagined Maggie in the pool, wearing a two-piece swimsuit that barely covered anything. The suit would probably be pink or yellow and she would have a towel to match when she emerged from the pool soaking wet, water falling from her neck to her breasts, moistening her—

"Grant!" Mavis whispered. "Come on!"

He stood at the screen door, impatiently pointing to inside the house. I pushed aside my

—memories, thoughts, fantasies—

And headed towards the house.

The kitchen was first. The moon gave us just enough light to see, even though everything had a dull white appearance to it.

Nothing strange in the kitchen. A few dishes needed cleaning and a bread package had been left open; a few pieces of the white bread spilled onto the counter top, but nothing particularly interesting.

We snuck down the hall. The walls held pictures of Maggie's mother and father and her older brother and his two sons. I remembered most of these pictures from previous visits. Now they seemed so far away from me in time and space.

"Grant," Mavis said in a normal volume, "we don't have time to reminisce about things."

I caressed the last picture on the wall of Maggie. In it, she sat on a rock at the Kankakee State Park, smiling and pointing to a large beaver that had climbed out of the water and headed towards her. She was excited that day, hoping the friendly beaver would make a good pet. We didn't find out; some kids pedaled by on bikes and scared the animal away.

More importantly, I had snapped the picture, and here it still hung. I wonder how Bobby felt about that.

I left the memories behind and joined Mavis in the living room. What I saw made me wish I still was thinking about my past with Maggie.

7

Blood spattered the walls above the couch and all along the wall to the front door. A huge glob of blood—dried now—lived right in the middle of the floor. The old tube TV had crashed to the floor, throwing shards of glass in every direction. The upturned coffee table leaned against the couch while the loveseat Maggie and I had debated for a week over buying had been sliced to shreds. This room, a complete mess.

Mavis and I could only stare for the moment.

"Holy shit," Mavis said finally.

"This is incredible," I managed.

"A disaster." Mavis sat on the arm of the Loveseat and closed his eyes.

"You okay?" I asked.

"Yeah, yeah. I'll be alright."

It hit me really quick. "Are you reminded of your parents?"

"Yes."

"Sorry, Mavis. Sorry this is the thing that had to remind you."

"Not your fault."

I nodded in agreement and let Mavis absorb the scene. "Who would do something like this? What individual was so angry at the world, at life, at Maggie that they turned this room into Hell?"

"Let's hope we can find out before it happens again," Mavis said, standing.

"I'm going upstairs," I said.

"'Kay."

I watched Mavis pilfer through the ripped Loveseat in search of something. Maybe he had an idea what he was looking for. I headed upstairs, not knowing what I sought.

On the way up, the dark forced a gloomy chill through my body. Whether that was from being dark or the result of the previous events, I didn't know. What I knew was I suddenly found myself wishing to be anywhere but here. I'd rather be in that cell right about now.

I quickly recalled how the upstairs was laid out: bathroom immediately to the right; a small bedroom past that, also on the right; and Maggie's bedroom on the left; at the end of the hall, a storage closet.

Maggie's bedroom door stood ajar by inches and I grabbed the edge and lightly shoved it inward. A tiny *thwang* let me know the door hit the stop and would go no further.

The room was neat, which didn't surprise me. Maggie had always been a neat freak, to put it mildly. Not anal, just tidy. The pink and yellow bedding looked untouched, so whatever happened occurred downstairs before she went to bed. A quick scan of the room elicited the same kind of order: alphabetized books on six shelves; an extremely neat desk with one can for pencils and one can for pens; the computer cords at the back of the desk neatly tied in sections with zip-ties; and even the pictures sticking to the vanity mirror were arranged in a perfect column on each side.

No wonder she was an excellent office manager. So organized and efficient. She obviously remained consistent from her work to her personal life in the years her and I were apart.

The mattress slid back a few inches and I caught myself on one of the posts.

I cried. The alarm clock ticked over three minutes and in that time, I didn't stop crying. I suddenly felt empty and out of control, like I stood on a cliff hundreds of feet up, and down below, a whirlpool lake yawned, inviting me to leap over the edge and whisk all this behind. I could imagine spinning every which way and becoming atrociously dizzy, wishing that when I slammed into the water at an astronomical speed that I would die. That break through the plane of the water was the passage into the world of no pain. No memory of bad things. No memory of Maggie being murdered.

Of Death.

"Grant!" Mavis' voice bordered on a scream. "Come down here."

After wiping my eyes, I snapped back to Maggie's room. I stood in the doorway.

I gave the room one last pass and almost overlooked something sticking out between the mattress and boxspring. I went back over and left the mattress up slightly, then retrieved the item.

It was a manila folder. On the tab, Maggie had written: 'FEATURE STORY'.

I flipped open the folder. The first page was a cover letter addressed to *The Ilton Gazette.*

"What were you doing, Maggie?"

The letter requested that I—as the editor—take a look at a feature story that Helen—as the writer—had written. The letter was addressed to me and said nothing else.

I pulled out a sheaf of lined paper that looked like a bunch of notes, all in Maggie's neat cursive handwriting. The notes contained locations, times and activities, but didn't say who the notes were about.

I came across the photos after fanning through the rest of the notes.

Most of the photographs were taken from a distance and contained the same main person in all of the pictures.

Chief of Police Bobby Hamilton.

Picture #1: Bobby was staking out Miss Molly's house.

Picture #2: Bobby entering Miss Molly's house. On the back of this picture was the date from the same day she died.

Picture #3: Taken from inside *Betty's Grubs*. Bobby sitting with Old Man Noonan, eating breakfast.

Picture #4-6: Bobby slipping something into Old Man Noonan's coffee.

Picture #7: About the only picture without Bobby. It was me cradling Noonan.

Picture after picture showed the same kind of thing: Bobby involved in the deaths of the past few weeks somehow. I couldn't look at any more pictures.

Something fell out when I went to close folder. A miniDV tape slapped against the floor. I picked it up. Written on the sticker, again in Maggie's handwriting, was 'PETE.'

My body tingled. I wanted to throw up, but I focused and the feeling subsided.

The thought of Pete's death being recorded did not help sustain the need to puke.

The headline read, 'LOCAL SERIAL KILLER DEVASTATES AREA WITH BRUTALITY'. Then, a subtitle: '*Suspect Exposed After Vigilante Investigation*'. Not the best choice for headlines; too emotional. The subtitle caught my attention better than the main headline.

The first paragraph implicated Bobby by name. I couldn't believe what I was reading. The photographs, this article. The next article was about other deaths in the area that couldn't be proved to be at Bobby's fault, but the suspicions were clear. One major death the article called out I remembered from a while ago. A man named Jerry Utny from the next town over disappeared and his body was pre-buried in a cemetery: the grave was dug and the body laid to rest in an open coffin. The killer was never found and the motive never determined.

"Grant!" I heard again. "What the hell are you doing up there?"

"Coming," I said. I tucked the tape in my pocket and closed the folder.

Downstairs, Mavis met me at the last step.

"You are not going to believe this," he said.

I followed him to the middle of the room and he stopped. "Do you see anything?" He asked.

Just like I had upstairs, I made a sweep of the living room and initially found nothing. "I don't, sorry. What am I looking for?"

He pointed to the couch. "Take a peek under that. I almost missed it myself."

I knelt down. A small piece of cloth stuck out from underneath. "Should I touch it?" I asked.

"Why not? I don't understand why this crime scene isn't secure. Whatever the case, they missed that."

"Bobby would love to find my fingerprints in here."

"I'm sure he would, but it's not going to matter once you see what it is." Mavis' voice rose to a near giddy level.

I pulled out the object. It was a hat. More of a cap really. The black cap had yellow trim lining the edge of the bill. An official police emblem sat dead center on the front of the cap, with Ilton stitched on the top part of the cloth badge and the motto, "Small Town, Big Hearts," written in cursive on the bottom, two words on either side of the point.

I turned it over and looked on the inside. On the size tag were initials in blue ink. 'B.H.' Inside the hat, near the tag were dots of blood that turned into a line of dried blood.

I said lowly, "You've got to be fucking kidding me."

"I don't think it can get any plainer than that."

"Maybe it was left here from a visit—"

"Don't be obtuse," Mavis said. "You know when this was left here."

"Yes, I do." I stared at the blood. "Whose blood do you think this is?"

"One of two people. Or maybe even two people."

"You've got to be fucking kidding me," I said again.

"What do you want to do?"

I really didn't know. I had three options. One, I could go to county police and tell them all we knew. The problem with that was did we have enough? Was a hat enough? The blood, the initials? So even if they took the hat and sent the blood off for analyzing, everyone would have to wait weeks for the results come back. Bobby could easily catch wind and foul everything up; or worse, disappear into the world. It was easy to do that these days if you knew the right people.

Two, I could confront Bobby. Every part of my brain knew that was a bad idea. All the reasoning inside me warned me not to endanger myself. If Bobby had killed Maggie then he would have no problem killing me or Mavis. Then, he'd go scot free. Of course, he might not be able to take me *and* Mavis or he could make a mistake and we could take him. Confrontation was possible but not viable.

Three, I could attempt to get Bobby to confess killing Maggie. That would be the hardest of the options because I had to assume he'd watch his words carefully and know what I was trying to pull.

"Mavis, I don't know. What do you think we should do?"

He thought intently for a moment, then said, "Let's go see Mr. Hamilton."

Option two, then.

8

On the way over, Mavis pointed to the car's glove compartment. "Open that up and take out the velvet bag."

I obeyed and undid the drawstring on the bag. I dumped the contents out and a revolver spilled onto my lap. Loose bullets followed.

"I haven't used one since my father taught me how to shoot," I said.

"Do you know how to load it?"

"Yes."

"You'll remember how to shoot it if you need to."

I slowly pushed each bullet into the empty hole in the six-bullet chamber. The metal of each bullet sounded like nails on a chalkboard to me. Six bullets, six nails on that chalkboard. I snapped the chamber shut and spun the revolver.

"Just like in the movies, isn't it?" Mavis commented.

"Yeah, but you know I'd rather rob a bank or protect the witness than go see Bobby in the middle of the night."

"It's all fucked up. I know that, you know that. How much more can you take?" Mavis turned down Bobby's street. "I mean, he arrested you!"

He slowed when he got a block from the house.

"You got the hat?" He asked.

I nodded.

"Good," Mavis said. "That's our leverage and bait."

"What is our plan?" I asked.

Mavis laughed. "Plan? Let's just show up and see what happens."

"He's going to flip when he sees me on his doorstep," I said.

"Element of surprise. Sometimes that's just as good a weapon as that gun there."

I weighed the gun in my hand. "But the weapon feels better."

Mavis parked the car across from Bobby's house. We waited a few minute to see if anything would happen and when nothing did, Mavis said, "Let's go."

On the way up, an upstairs light came on. Both Mavis and I paused in the middle of the front lawn. A silhouette walked by the window, then made a return pass. The light remained on. Mavis pointed to the bushes in front of the porch and we each took a position behind them on either side of stairs.

How much of a surprise did Mavis want to have? I lost sight of the window, so hopefully Mavis could see it. I desperately wanted Mavis to know what he was doing, but I suspected otherwise. How much experience did he have bullying someone into giving a confession of murder? His expertise was ghosts. Part of me wondered how well this was going to go, but another part of me wanted not to get involved. To let some other professional handle this business.

The longer we waited, the heavier the gun felt in my hands. I set it down on the ground to stretch my legs out when I heard Mavis emerge from his bush.

"The light is off," he whispered. "Come on."

As feathery as we could, we took the steps slowly one at a time. Despite the simple movement, I wanted to keel over in exhaustion. My calves protested any more movement, so to stall, I waited for Mavis to move forward first towards the front door.

You forgot the gun! My mind screamed. Dammit! It still rested behind the bush.

I heard the front door slowly open.

"Hello, guys." Bobby stood in his doorway, his standard issue police Glock aimed right for my head. He was dressed in his police uniform with a generic cap that said *Police* in yellow block lettering. "Come on in."

CHAPTER FOURTEEN

1

Running would have done no good. My hatred for Chief Bobby Hamilton grew strong and ran for years, but I didn't doubt the accuracy of his aim. The gun stayed firm in his hands and his eye contained a fix focus on the spot right on the bridge of my nose.

Mavis and I begrudgingly entered Bobby's house. I palmed no gun and Mavis had no plan. Bobby held the upper hand *and* the surprise Mavis had wanted.

Bobby stepped a safe distance from us and flicked his head in the direction of the living room. "In there," he said. "Sit."

We did, like schoolchildren forced to conform to the instructions of our elders.

"So I have an escaped prisoner and an outsider who is obstructing justice," Bobby said, following us. "This is my lucky day."

"What are you going to do? Arrest us?" Mavis asked.

"That's the backup plan," he answered.

Mavis didn't ask any other questions. We both knew what the main plan was.

"Grant, the hat," Mavis said to me.

Bobby moved the muzzle of the gun from me to Mavis and then back to me when I reach for my right pocket. At first, I didn't feel the hat back there and wondered for a second if it fell out when I hid behind the bush. Gun and hat, in a strange matrimony of my future demise, living out the rest of their days in front of Bobby's house.

Mavis opened his eyes and I read a little fear into them. I concentrated and my butt gave me the answer. *The other pocket, moron.* I felt the bulge on my left buttock and breathed a very small sigh of relief. Maybe this would get us a few more minutes.

"What the fuck are you doing?" Bobby took a step closer to me. I'm sure he thought I was removing a gun.

"No gun, just a hat," I said. The quiver in my voice disappointed me. No doubt, Bobby heard it. I sensed the delight and slowly brought the hat around for him to see.

"What's that?" He asked the question, but his face gave him away. The gun faltered for a split second, but he quickly caught himself and popped it back in line to me. Bobby knew exactly what this was.

And I could tell he knew it was his.

"I do believe," Mavis said, "that is your hat."

"Please, how can I believe that? Looks like any old cop's hat." Bobby kept trying to get a closer look at the hat, just to make sure it really "looked like any old cop's hat."

Stubborn little fucker, I thought.

I turned the hat around so he could see the emblem. At once, he recognized it.

"Do I need to prove it any further?" I flipped the hat over and used my finger to extend the tag into the open. "B.H. Now who the hell could that be?"

Bobby grunted some anger and held out his free hand. "Give that here."

"There's something else," I said, the confidence returning to my voice. I pointed to the blood and said, "I can't tell whose blood this is. I have a couple of theories, but would you happen to know?"

"That is now stolen police property," he said.

Mavis laughed. "Not if it's found at a crime scene. Does the name Maggie ring a bell?"

For a moment, I seriously thought Bobby would give this all up. I thought he would hand the gun over, say I'm sorry and let us take him to County. Maybe he'd cry, maybe he'd show no emotion or maybe he'd want mercy. The serene look that washed over his face misled me, of course. I realized when he formed a crooked smirk that things were going to go haywire.

Bobby turned his body halfway towards Mavis and removed the gun from my vicinity and pointed it at Mavis.

"Of course that little bitch's name rings a bell," he said.

He pulled the trigger. The *crack* of the gun sucked out all the air in my body. Mavis flew back against the couch, holding his side. Ribs? Lungs? Stomach? Blood seeped through his clothes and spread quickly. I couldn't tell what the bullet hit and how severe the gunshot was.

Bobby returned the gun to me. "I'll take that hat."

He moved to me and got maybe two steps when I saw Mavis jump on Bobby's back. Like a crazy, angry Chimpanzee, Mavis wrapped Bobby in a chokehold, but tried to use both arms at the same time. This idea was correct, just not the technique. Still, it gave me time to leap up and plow Bobby in a mid-section tackle

—bobby had some abs 8 minute abs—

and drive him back into the foyer wall.

Mavis yelped and Bobby gasped as the air left his lungs. Bobby reached back and gripped Mavis' shirt and tugged him to the side and I saw Mavis go rolling towards the inner hallway.

Bobby brought his knee to my chin and my teeth rattled. My eyes watered immediately. I had never been kicked in the face. Punched, yes, but a knee to the chin was a definitely worse experience. Warm blood dripped from my lip as I tried to move my lower jaw.

I staggered backwards, feeling for anything to grab onto. My hands didn't find anything and I fell backwards to the floor. As I did, I glanced at Mavis crawling away.

Bobby straightened and looked at both of us, deciding who he would go after first.

Mavis was the choice.

"Bobby! Why did you kill all the others!" I yelled. With my jaw in excruciating pain, I didn't think my words were audible. It worked; Bobby stopped and turned to me.

"Others?" he said. "What others?" He raised his gun. "There were no others." The sarcasm in his voice made me cringe.

"Sure there was," I said. "Miss Molly, Pete, Betty. Even Old Man Noonan. What the fuck is wrong with you?" Molly came out 'olly' and Pete came out 'ete.' Some of my hard consonants weren't getting through.

Bobby fired one shot into my shoulder. Searing heat migrated from the bullet hole through my right shoulder and into my armpit. With each pump of my heart, the pain continuously swelled in gobs. I screamed. Who cares if Bobby thought I was a wimp; it fucking hurt!

"Everything is *unwrong* with me, Grant. It's everyone else who is all fucked up. You, Mavis, everyone that died. The world is full of fucked up people from here to Goddamn China. Is there no place in this world that one can live without fucked up people fucking it up?" Bobby smiled. "Nowhere, but sometimes the world just needs someone to step forward and take initiative."

"And that someone is you, I take it."

"At the moment. This position was bestowed on me and I cannot let anyone down. I take it very seriously, as you can probably tell." He tightened his grip on the gun and I already saw the path of the bullet. Like a horrendously highlighted piece of string, the path loomed before me. My heart jumped.

"How long?" I asked.

"How long what?"

"How long have you been doing this?"

Bobby shook his head. "What do you mean by 'long'? How long have *I* been doing this? Or how long has my family been doing this?"

Family? That was one fact of the article that I didn't catch. I played over everything that I read in that folder and I couldn't recall information that said anything about a 'family' doing this.

"I don't understand. What would your family have to do with this?" I said.

"Years, Grant. Over seventy years my father, Grandfather and I have been helping the fucked up people of the world find another world to fuck up. I'm pretty sure Hell likes fucked up people. And I like sending fucked up people to hell. But do you know the hardest part? Trying to frame you. Planting the evidence so you'd question yourself was easy—don't think I didn't know you took the hairbrush and the tape recorder—even starting the rumors in town was pretty simple. The hardest part was acting like you, making Miss Molly think I was you. I covered my face and entered her home under the pretext of a reporter. In the end, I just acted like a stupid reporter." Bobby eyed up his aim again and said, "What does it matter? You are fucked up and are going to move on."

"Did Maggie deserve it? Did she deserve the punishment you *bestowed* on her?"

"She deserved it more than anyone in all of my family's years of doing this."

A gunshot shouted through the room. My eyes instinctively slammed shut, but I felt no other pain besides the one in my shoulder.

I opened them and saw Bobby ducking and keeping an eye on the front window. A bullet hole sat in the center of the window and, following the trajectory of the bullet, I caught sight of a hole in the wall behind where Bobby had stood. A trail of blood followed Bobby to the front door.

Mavis must have found the gun I left behind.

Standing up too quick, my head became woozy and I halted moving until it passed. Luckily, that took only a couple seconds.

2

Bobby was already down the porch stairs when I reached the open front door. He searched the front yard and when he didn't see anything, he turned back to me with an irritated scowl and sprinted towards me. When he reached the top step, which was only three feet from me, he raised his gun and said, "Alright Grant, time to be a shitty editor in Hell now."

"Don't," Mavis said behind him. He held up the revolver with confidence in his left hand, even though his right hand cupped the gunshot wound. From the spot he covered, it only appeared to be a side wound, with no major organ hit. If we didn't get this over with soon, he could lose a detrimental amount of blood.

Bobby continued to face me. "And if I don't?" He muttered.

"I don't know; why don't you try and test me." Mavis coughed once and he brought the gun hand to his face to cover the mouth. He coughed twice more.

"There's no need for me to test you," Bobby said.

Keeping his eyes on me, Bobby used the muzzle of the gun to peel pack the collar of his police-issued shirt. It creased until the top bottom. Underneath the shirt was a Kevlar jacket.

Bobby smiled.

"Mavis!" I yelled. "He's got—!"

A piercing scream shot through the air, causing all three of us to cup our ears for protection. The banshee was near, but where?

Darting his eyes around, Bobby scanned the area, but didn't see anything.

But I did. Mavis did.

The banshee appeared on our right, emerging from behind a house. She floated quickly across the yard and entered the street with dazzling speed. A look on her face indicated she was after someone. Me? Mavis? Bobby?

Bobby spun around and raised his gun to shoot Mavis in the face. Unfortunately for Bobby, Mavis had ducked, kneeling on one knee as Bobby's gun went off. The bullet raced through the woman, causing a smoky hole to materialize, ricocheting off of a tree and disappearing into the night. A stunned Bobby took two seconds too long to be shocked from missing Mavis.

While I heard Mavis' revolver fire, I'm pretty sure the bullet missed Bobby by a few inches and landed by my foot, splattering cement shards into my leg.

I went to the ground, grasping my ankle.

The banshee passed Mavis and stopped directly in front of Bobby. I was positive he didn't know what to do, but the banshee did.

She started to dissipate and each molecule or cell or little dot of her began surrounding Bobby. It was at this point that he thought he could move, but when he tried, his feet remained planted to the ground. The swirling mist rotated around Bobby in a supernatural orbit at his feet, slowly moving upwards to his knees, waist and torso. Bobby turned his head as far as he could go to try to look at me, but I was on the ground, ready for whatever would happen next.

I heard a loud *whooooooosh* and the banshee's essence circled Bobby's head.

"Nooooo! Aaaaaaagh! Aaaaa—" Bobby's last proclamation was cut short from the massive amount of the mist diving into his mouth. A quick choke and Bobby's body spasmed, collapsed and finally disappeared. If I wasn't there to see it, I wouldn't have believed it. The ground *absorbed* Bobby's body.

Bobby and the banshee were gone.

Mavis and I waited a few minutes before standing. I was okay. The pain in my shoulder lessened, most likely from the adrenaline, but when Mavis tried to rise, he collapsed. If we both didn't get some sort of medical attention, we'd be fucked. Mavis more than I.

"Shit!" I screamed.

I ran to him and helped him to his feet.

"Let's get to your car," I said.

He nodded and let me guide him to the passenger seat. It was slow moving and I thought we'd never get to the car. I found an old coat in the back seat and I grabbed it and handed it to him.

"Use this to push on the wound. Slow the bleeding at least. The nearest hospital is twenty minutes away, and that's speeding."

"Okay."

When I got into driver's seat and started the car, he grabbed onto my arm.

"Thank you," he said.

I gave him a questioning gaze. "For what? It's you I should be thanking."

"For leaving that gun in the bushes."

I laughed. "Believe me, I didn't do it on purpose."

"I know. It seemed to be serendipity."

"You're going to hurt yourself using big words."

"Then get your ass moving and drive to a hospital."

And that's exactly what I did.

Epilogue

One Week Later

Maggie's funeral was nice. A simple affair with most of Ilton attending, as well as her closest family. Some of her family members, I learned, were abroad and couldn't get here in time and her mother and father wanted to get it over with. It was bad enough she died the way she did, they said, but to let her soul linger on was worse than that.

I had no more strange nightmares or weird little dreams about my family and I didn't see the banshee again, so I was pretty sure all of that was completed.

Mavis stayed in town a few days after the funeral, just to make sure everything with Ex-Police Chief Bobby Hamilton was finished. The file and the tape were turned over to county and with Bobby dead, there was no reason to waste taxpayer's money to finalize the investigation. Mavis claimed that if it did go on, I'd probably write a feature story about it, exposing this and exposing that. No one trusted a reporter anymore.

It's an understatement to say that the town was devastated by the recent events. I received many apologies and requests to continue to edit the *Ilton Gazette*, but I felt a need to move on. Running the paper would not be the same without Pete or Maggie there. Time to go on to something bigger or take a break or go somewhere far away from here. They understood and Jerry would probably get the job. The paper would still get printed, so nothing to worry about there.

On my last day in town, one week after Maggie's funeral, I met Mavis at *Betty's* for one last lunch. Bittersweet for sure, but I couldn't just leave.

With a coffee and hamburger platter in front of me and a chicken lunch special in front of Mavis, we shook hands.

"It seems this town is going to miss you," he said.

"I know, but I can't be here any longer."

"I understand."

We took a couple of bites, enjoying the greasiness of it all. "I will miss this," I said, using my fork to point to my food.

"Dive food is the best."

"Hey now, don't disrespect it."

We laughed. We laughed for a long time, letting the stress of the past few weeks roll away into this moment. This was the moment we both knew would end when our food was gone. When we would walk out the door, get into our separate cars and continue on with our lives in different places.

Sometimes, people bonded over disasters like this, and neither of us said it after everything was done, but there would be no point in staying in contact. Mavis the ghosthunter and I the editor. We knew there would be no point and no doubt that soon, these events would just be a memory to give us nightmares.

"I'm sorry about the banshee," I said.

"What do you mean?"

"You didn't get to catch it or research it or whatever it is you do." More food.

He waved the statement away with his hand. "No matter. I understand that she was trying to help. She gave us so many warnings, how were we to know, right?"

The reporter surfaced. "What about your parents? What about what happened to mine? Are you still curious about it all?"

"No. I've pretty much wasted my life on this and it's time to move on."

I nodded.

Mavis had decided moved on. The banshee had moved on.

We finished our lunch, paid our bill and procrastinated by our cars passing chit-chat between us.

"Listen, I hate to be the one to say it," I said, "but you realize we are dilly-dallying."

"Yeah, I know."

"You've been a good friend through all of this."

"You too."

"It's for the best, this."

"It is for the best, I can't argue with that."

We hugged, broke and got into our cars. I watched him back out and pull away before I did the same, heading for the northern edge of town.

I stopped at the very last crossroad leading out of town and pulled to the side of the road. I checked my rearview mirror and mentally said goodbye to the town that gave me everything when I was growing up and everything when I came back. I returned once and I wasn't going to return again.

It was time to move on.

ACKNOWLEDGEMENTS

Any book ever written is not a solo affair. A writer's life is somewhat solitary, but eventually, that rough draft must reach some other person's eyes or you have to reach out to an expert for research. *Nightcry* was not a solo affair. I would like to thank my wife, Nancy, first and foremost for giving me the support to get this thing done. She's been an integral part in giving me the time to finish this novel and my subsequent works.

Others I'd like to thank: my Beta readers Michelle Sussman and Andrew Saxsma. I'd also like to thank my general Beta readers Rikki Goodwin and Michael Sander, who tirelessly read my short stories and novels, taking the time to give me constructive criticism.

Also, thank you, Mr. and Ms. Reader. By purchasing this book you have given me that chance to creep you out or scare you or—at the very least—make you check over your shoulder to see if anyone or anything is sneaking up on you.

The Golden Door

Chapter One

June 20

Adam didn't want to go into his mother's bedroom, but she had asked for him. He knew death hovered like a balloon over his mother, its lips probably smacking with giddy delight. He placed his sweaty and shaking palm around the doorknob anyway and twisted, hoping the door, the room behind it and the impending doom would disappear around him. Fourteen was too young to be without a mother.

After lightly shoving the door inward, Adam took a step inside the bedroom. The avalanche of smells made him cringe and he covered his mouth with his right hand to keep his lunch down. Beer was the immediate and instantly recognizable smell. Adam noticed his father slumped in an old, brown La-Z-Boy recliner with a bottle of beer hanging from his fingertips. Adam wondered when his father last took a shower. His father's oily hair shone in the light of dusk and dark smudges of dirt or grease or whatever it was pressed deep into the cracks in his aging face.

The vibrating snores of his father shook the arm holding the bottle and Adam expected the bottle to fall to its death at any moment. Like a dutiful son, Adam considered removing the bottle, then tossed the thought aside. *What if he wakes up and wants a beer really bad and remembers he had a bottle in his hand when he went to sleep and when he lifts his hand to take sip, it won't be there and then he'll be angry and want you to get a tree branch for switchin' time. No, better just to leave it there.*

A deep, rotten meat scent was the second smell. Adam sniffed the air again and he recalled the time he didn't finished washing the dishes and they sat out for days. During that time, the food left behind quickly rotted and contaminated the air with a hollow, biting stench that tattled on Adam when his father came home the day his accident happened at the factory. Adam never forgot to wash the dishes again.

Much to the surprise of Adam, a third smell caressed his nose. *Rose petals*, Adam guessed. The scent hung in the air between the other two disgusting smells. Adam stepped in further and noticed an oval decanter of perfume sitting on the nightstand. *Silent Rose* was stamped on the sticker affixed to the front side. Adam and Tommy had pooled their money together last year and got the perfume for her birthday. The perfume cost them $12 and they just had enough and they knew it wasn't going to be like the stuff you see J-Lo or Britney Spears selling, but their mother always told them when you give gifts, don't worry about what you get because it's the thought that counts. And she wore it almost every day.

It's the thought that counts.

"Ad—" His mother's voice cracked. It didn't sound healthy. She let loose with a cough and turned her head towards Adam. "Adam. You are here."

"I am, mother."

"Come here." She paused to catch her breath. "I want to talk to you."

Adam glanced at his father and walked across the bedroom when he thought it was safe. In case his father suddenly woke up and caught Adam in the bedroom, Adam had a quick plan of escape: dive under the bed. His father frowned upon Adam and his brother constantly visiting their mother during her sickness. *She'll never get better if you two shitbirds keep buggin' her*, he'd say.

Adam didn't acknowledge his mother until he stood next to the bed in order to focus all his power on being stealthy.

"How are you feeling?" Adam asked. Really, it was a stupid question, he knew. The sickness has lived in her for nine months. Nine months tomorrow, to be exact. Adam looked at the floor; how silly could he be for tallying the days?

"I'm dying Adam. This cancer has been eating me alive for a year." A cough. "I am ready to leave this place."

"No. You just need some rest."

"I'll be getting plenty of that soon."

A rough grunt came from the corner. Adam watched his father shift slightly in the chair, the bottle of beer still secure.

"Adam, come closer. I want to tell you something." His mother tried to move so her whole body faced him, but he stopped her.

"Mom, no. Just stay still." Adam leaned in. "What do you want to say?"

"It's about your father."

"What about him?"

"I want you to be wary of him."

"Wary? What does that mean?"

"Keep an eye on him."

Adam nodded. "Of course. Tom and I will take care of him."

"I didn't mean—" Another cough. "I didn't mean like that. You and your brother need to watch out for him. He's not a pleasant person."

"I don't understand."

A weak hand emerged from under the covers and lightly touched Adam's cheek. Adam enjoyed the quick contact from his mother, even though it took a good amount of effort from her.

"Don't trust him," his mother said. "Ever."

His mother scooted up, but she struggled. She placed her arms under her body to hoist what she could, but Adam saw the trouble she was having. Adam got his arms under her back and lifted and pulled her toward the headboard.

When his mother was propped against the headboard and regained some of her strength back, she said, "You're strong. You should play some sports when you become a sophomore this school year."

"I've been thinking about it."

His mother reached over and slowly lowered the shoulder part of her nightgown. This motion revealed a three or four-inch gash oozing blood. The edges of the cut had started to turn black and small flakes of older blood slipped onto his mother's fresher skin.

"Your father did that to me weeks ago," she said. "It has never healed properly." She returned the sleeve back to her shoulder. "Not that it matters now, anyway," his mother added.

"He would never hurt *us*," Paul said.

"I know he won't," she said.

With some of her last strength, his mother reached over with both hands and cupped Adam's face. "I'll make sure of that," she said.

"How?"

"Don't worry about that. You worry about your summer; you worry about getting ready for the next school year; you worry about girls; you worry about everything else besides how I'll make sure your father doesn't hurt you." His mother looked over to his father and then continued. "I'm making you a promise right now that he won't and that I will make his life a living hell."

Adam shook his head. "But why? I know he won't hurt us."

"You can't be sure, Adam."

"Neither can you, mom. You're too weak."

"Though the body is weak," his mother said, "the will is strong."

"I don't want you to promise that. I want you to promise you won't die."

Adam saw sympathy shoot from his mother's eyes. *Why is she giving* me *the sympathy?* At that moment he knew she couldn't promise that, but hoped the next words out of her mouth would be just that.

"I am human and the cancer is beyond my control." She slid back down into the bed and this was easier for her. Adam made an attempt to help her, but his mother shook her head. "You are a sweet boy, Adam. Soon, the girls will be begging you to make them happy."

"Mom…" Adam sensed tears welling, bulking up like a clogged drain that didn't want to be unclogged.

"Don't cry. Give me a hug."

Adam raised his arms and intertwined them with his mother's arms. They embraced for a minute as Adam soaked in every ounce of love his mother released. Adam realized this is the last hug he would receive from his mother and the tears flowed. His mother patted the back of Adam's head.

"I love you, Adam."

"I love you too, mom."

She gave him a final squeeze and Adam pulled away. "I have to rest now," she said.

Defeated, Adam stepped back. His mother relaxed her head, her eyes gazing toward the ceiling. Adam watched his mother's eyes roll up into her head.

This is it, Adam thought. *I'm going to watch her die.* He wished his father was awake and Tommy was standing here also. Really, he only wanted Tommy next to him. Adam wondered why his mother had just called him and not Tommy too. Wasn't she also afraid of his father waking up or worse, pretending to be asleep and hearing everything they said? He would be angry and ready to do some *switching*. But his father didn't wake and Tommy wasn't here; he was forced to watch his mother die.

He was forced to do it alone.

A light gasp escaped his mother's mouth. Her lips vibrated for a split second and then her head lolled to the right, facing Adam. The eyes remained open, but no life remained. Adam took a step towards her to close the eyelids, but stopped. He didn't want to give his father any reason to think he'd been in the bedroom.

With no other reason to stay in the room, Adam turned and caught a glimpse of his father. For a second, Adam thought his father *had* awakened and watched him behind blurry and inebriated eyes. *Hey son, whatch ya guys talkin' about over there? Havin' a little mother-son talk about stuff? Well, tell me this stuff, eh son? Your good ole involved father wants to know this stuff. If you don't start tellin' me what you and your whore mother were talkin about, I'm goin' to have you pick out a nice little branch for a wonderful switchin' time!*

This was not the case though: his father choked on a snore and continued sleeping.

Adam relaxed.

Sneaking across the floor to leave the room just as he had to reach his mother, Adam made it to the bedroom door without incident. His father stayed sleeping; the beer continued to hang perilously over the floor; and the Death Scent hit Adam even harder as he passed through the doorway into the hall. The Scent became stronger somehow since the passing of his mother.

Adam quietly shut the door and went into the bathroom. The lock to this door was broken and Adam pushed the clothes hamper in front of the door. After swiping the shower curtain back, Adam stepped into the tub and sat down. He just needed a few minutes.

The few minutes turned into thirty as he let fly all of the tears.

Out now: www.nightcrynovel.com

Made in the USA
Columbia, SC
26 July 2018